QUEST OF HONOR

SEARCHING HEARTS

BOOK ONE

ELLIE ST. CLAIR

Facebook: Ellie St. Clair

Cover by AJF Designs

Do you love historical romance? Receive access to a free ebook, as well as exclusive content such as giveaways, contests, freebies and advance notice of pre-orders through my mailing list!

Sign up here!

Also By Ellie St. Clair

Searching Hearts
Duke of Christmas (prequel)
Quest of Honor
Clue of Affection
Hearts of Trust
Hope of Romance
Promise of Redemption

Searching Hearts Box Set (Books 1-5)

For a full list of all of Ellie's books, please see
www.elliestclair.com/books.

CONTENTS

PROLOGUE

arie set her fork and knife down, sitting back to contentedly run her gaze over her five children – until it came to rest upon Thomas. Normally she was most concerned about Daniel, her eldest and the next in line to assume the title of Duke, but there was something about Thomas tonight that seemed off to her.

Typically rather jovial, this evening he wore a frown that bothered her, and had taken on the brooding silence that overcame him whenever he felt stifled or frustrated.

The remainder of her children, from Daniel at twenty-four down to her sixteen-year-old daughter Polly, were chattering away as they were normally wont to do, no matter how she tried to instill in them the proper etiquette of the dinner hour. Her husband, Lionel, known to most as the Duke of Ware, sat in his usual place at the head of the table, intent on his meal as he listened to the stories of his brood.

"Thomas," Marie finally said, to which he raised his dark head, "is everything quite well, darling?"

"Yes, Mother," he replied quickly.

"Are you quite sure?"

"Well… since you asked," he said, looking hesitantly at her and then his father. "I do have something of an announcement."

Marie raised her eyebrows as the chatter around the table hushed, Thomas' nerves apparent to them all.

"I am going to be joining His Majesty's Navy," he finally said, puffing his chest out, sitting up straight and setting back his shoulders.

"The Navy!" Marie exclaimed incredulously as her stomach dropped, hoping that he was jesting but knowing from his face that he was fully committed to his pronouncement. "You cannot be serious."

"I am Mother," he responded, setting his jaw as a chill that Marie did not appreciate stole over his voice. "The Navy is a noble profession. Besides, what else am I to do with my life?"

"You are the second son of a duke. What if you need to assume the title and you are injured or dead somewhere at sea?"

"Are you wishing for my death, Mother?" Daniel said from down the table, amusement edging the growl of his voice.

Polly snickered before Thomas shot her a look and started in again.

"I shall not spend my life sitting here in case of Father and Daniel's deaths, Mother," he responded, his voice becoming slightly more heated, although Marie knew he would never fully raise it at her. "In the meantime, I am ready to see beyond England's shores."

"You can tour the continent."

"And the rest of the world? It is all out there waiting for me, Mother. What better way to see it all than on the sea?"

Marie lifted a hand to her forehead, rubbing her brow. She knew Thomas was a grown man, and yet she still hated the thought of one of her children in such danger.

"Lionel!" she finally attempted, turning to her husband fervently. "Have you nothing to say?"

Lionel finished chewing his potatoes, crossing his arms over his chest as he fixed his gaze on his son, one of his dark eyebrows raised.

"Well, son," he said. "I would say your intentions are admirable. Do you completely understand what you are getting yourself into?"

"I do."

"Well, then, I'd best talk to my friend the Admiral tomorrow. The son of the Duke of Ware must find a reasonable berth and vessel upon which to serve."

Thomas' face lit up as Marie's heart sank. She fixed her husband with a stare to tell him she had much more to say on the subject, but he caught her eye and lifted a shoulder, telling her what she knew – that Thomas was far too old to keep under her wing, and she had no choice but to let him go.

That didn't mean she had to be happy about it.

She saw Violet, her eldest daughter, smile encouragingly at Thomas, and she sighed, knowing that she was outnumbered.

"Thank you, Father," Thomas said. "I would most appreciate it."

"This is quite ridiculous," Marie said with one last attempt at reasoning with Thomas, her head swivelling from her son to Lionel and back to Thomas once more. "Thomas is twenty-two years old! He and Daniel should be finding wives, settling down, raising children. Instead, Daniel is out doing heaven knows what and Thomas will be at sea miles away from us. How is it that I have three children of marriageable age, none of whom have any interest in actually being married?"

She didn't miss Benjamin and Polly smirk at the fact they

3

were not included in her plea, and she held out hope that one day they would listen to her, even if the other three refused.

"In due time, Mother," said Violet, somewhat mollifying her, "in due time. In the meantime, let us drink to Thomas and the world that awaits him."

"To Thomas!" They all joined in – even Marie, begrudgingly – and as Thomas grinned, she knew her son would never be the same man he was again.

CHAPTER 1

FIVE YEARS LATER

*E*leanor Adams sat primly on one of the room's two straight-backed chairs as her father stomped around, muttering unintelligible ramblings under his breath. She waited patiently for his judgement to fall, knowing that he would not be able to bring himself to punish her too severely. She was, after all, his only child, and he had never been able to be too strict with her.

"You cannot simply do as you please, Eleanor!" her father sputtered, his complexion having altered to beetroot red. "What if we had not seen you?"

Eleanor stifled a sigh of frustration. "Papa, you know me better than that. I simply *had* to investigate what was down there." A small smile crept across her face. "And, if I had not, then we would not currently have these three small trunks in our possession." She swept her hand out toward the three still damp trunks that sat beside her father's desk, glancing at them triumphantly before returning her gaze to her father.

To her very great relief, he sighed and sat down heavily behind his desk, although he continued to shake his head at her.

"We have not opened them yet, Eleanor," her father said, a little gruffly. "You could have risked your life for nothing."

In response, Eleanor tossed her head, aware of the spots of moisture that shook off her long hair, which was hanging loose around her shoulders. "I am one of the best swimmers among the crew, Papa. You know that."

"But still," he retorted, "you cannot just dive off the ship without alerting someone to what you have found! Had you done so, I could have dropped the anchor and gone to see what was there."

Eleanor bit her lip, aware that her father was being more than reasonable. Had any one of his crew done what she had, they would have been severely punished; as the captain's daughter, she had been chastised – as had the crew.

Her cheeks warmed, primarily at the knowledge that she had caused trouble for the men. "I was trying to prove myself, Papa," she explained, more quietly. "As the only woman on board, I have to take extra steps to show my worth."

His face softened. "Eleanor, you already have my respect and the respect of the crew. For over twenty years, you have traveled the seas with us, and you have no need to prove yourself now. Doing such a thing is both dangerous and shows a lack of regard for me — not only as your father, but also as your captain." His lined face grew more serious, as his bushy eyebrows clung together. "You know that I will need to punish you for what you did, Eleanor. As much as it pains me to do this, you are to be confined to your quarters for two days."

"Two days?" Eleanor gasped, staring at her father. "But I will miss the exploration!"

Her father nodded gravely. "I have to show the crew that I am not afraid to punish you, even though you are my daughter." A hint of a smile pulled up the corner of his lips. "Just be glad it is not the cat o' nine tails, Eleanor."

Eleanor sagged against the chair, her ladylike position gone in a moment. Reflecting on her father's decision, she had to admit that it was fair, lenient even. She had acted impulsively, as she was wont to do. She had seen the glistening below the surface and had dived in before thinking it through. Although, in hindsight, had she alerted anyone she may have avoided the trouble but she certainly would not have been chosen to investigate.

"I am sorry you will miss the exploration of the Blackmoor Caves," her father continued, gently. "But Eleanor, you must know that you cannot simply do what you please on this ship."

"I do know, Papa," Eleanor replied, duly, annoyed with herself, for instead of proving herself as a sailor, she was now being treated as a child. She could only hope the treasure would yield results that would make all forget about the find and focus on the outcome. "I'm sorry."

Her father placed a gentle hand on her shoulder, getting to his feet with a grunt. "Like you say, however, we have retrieved three trunks."

Hope sparked in Eleanor's chest. "You mean, I can open them?"

He chuckled, finally releasing his angry tension. He never stayed mad at her for long. "I think so. After all, you were the one who spotted the locks gleaming under the ocean's waves."

Eleanor rose, her booted feet clattering across the wooden floor of the cabin as she made her way toward the trunks. She had to change into dry clothing, but that could wait. "It is only because we are in such shallow waters," she said, bending down to examine the trunks. "Had the water been any deeper, then I doubt we would have found them."

"Here." Her father handed her a large mallet, and, using all her strength, Eleanor swung it back and then forward to hit the first lock.

It broke easily, evidently having been underwater for some time. With bated breath, Eleanor pushed the top of the trunk back. A wide grin slowly spread across her face as her eyes roved over the bounty.

"There is some gold here," she said, pulling out a coin and handing it to her father. "Not much, but enough."

Chuckling, her father picked up the mallet and broke the other two locks, finding more gold and some silver in the other two trunks. He crowed with delight as he grasped great handfuls of coins, letting them trickle back down through his fingers and into the trunk. Despite her impending punishment, Eleanor could not help but smile too, delighted that they would have more than enough to pay the crew for the next quarter.

"Everyone shall have a bonus!" her father declared, getting to his feet and throwing open the door to his cabin. "Morgan!"

The first mate came stumbling in, as though he'd been waiting for the captain to call his name. "Aye, Captain Adams?"

Eleanor grinned as her father slapped Morgan on the back, before gesturing toward the treasure.

"Here," he said, "sort this out. Crew's pay and a bonus for everyone. Leave the first trunk, take the other two."

Morgan returned Eleanor's smile, and got to the task at once, jubilant over some of the wonders he was finding. It would take him an age to sort out the treasure into piles of equal worth, but Eleanor knew it was a job the first mate thoroughly enjoyed.

Wiping her hands down the front of her breeches, Eleanor rose to her feet and smiled at her father, wondering if he might forget her punishment.

Unfortunately, he had not.

"Right, Eleanor, to your cabin now. Your meals will be sent down."

A sigh left her lips as she trudged past him, sniffing inelegantly. Behind her, she heard her father's soft chuckle.

"Two days will be over before you know it, my dear," he said, following her out. "And if we find anything at the caves, you may join in the salvaging."

That was a slight relief, causing her shoulders to rise from their slumped position. "Thank you, Papa," she mumbled, as the fresh air hit her lungs. Taking in another few breaths, Eleanor took in the smell of the sea, the wind whipping at her hair...before she realized that the entire crew was watching her.

Taking a breath, she lifted her chin. "I should not have dived off the ship without alerting someone to what I had found," she said, loudly. "I did you all wrong by acting so impulsively and showed disrespect to our captain. I will not do such a thing again." She caught the look of sympathy in some of the crew members' eyes, although they appeared to be relieved that she was receiving some kind of punishment. There were some men she knew, though they would never say it aloud, who were not particularly pleased with her presence on the ship. Without another word, Eleanor turned on her heel and walked down the short staircase to her cabin below.

Being the only woman meant she had one of only two tiny cabins that were located below deck — Morgan, the first mate, held the other. Pulling open the door, she looked glumly into her gloomy room, hating that she would be stuck inside for two days.

"Thank you for your apology, Eleanor," her father said, holding the door as she walked inside. "The crew respects you, as they do me. They will hold you in greater esteem because you have confessed your wrongs."

Eleanor tried to smile, sitting down on the small bed. "Thank you, Papa. I believe the treasure I found for them may also have increased their sense of 'esteem' of me."

He grinned at her. "You're a pirate's daughter, Eleanor. Some might think that means we have no standards, no way of keeping control, but you know how precarious the sea — and the crew — can be. They are loyal to me, and I want them to be loyal to you too. One day, this ship could be yours." With a quick smile, he closed the door and left her to her thoughts.

Eleanor stared at the door, her father's words echoing around her mind. One day, she might have control of the ship? Was he serious? It was the first time he had ever mentioned such an idea, and while she didn't want to raise her hopes, the thought had her heart beating faster.

Eleanor knew that in the Navy, there would be no thought of having a female captain, nor even a female crew member, but they were far removed from any legitimate naval operation. Pirates did things differently and, if her father thought the crew would respect her as the captain, then she would gladly step into the role, though she hoped it would be some time before her father gave it up and retired from the seas.

A pirate captain. The thought made her smile, despite her current punishment. To roam the seas at the helm of the ship with her crew, searching for bounty and, in their case, helping those less fortunate. She could not think of a better life.

CHAPTER 2

*C*aptain Thomas Harrington sat back and rubbed his temples as he studied the newly drawn poster of the pirate captain. It was as good a portrait as he could expect, he supposed, given that he had not seen the man in some time, and even then, it had been a fleeting glimpse.

Since then, the man had remained just out of his grasp, although he couldn't be too concerned, for no one else had managed to capture him either – as the reward slowly grew.

"It will do," he said dismissively. "Ensure they are placed around all the local ports."

He turned to the printer's errand boy who had delivered the drawing, noting his youth and hopeful demeanor, recognizing himself when he had first entered this life. The young man nodded before stepping out of the room.

Releasing a sigh, Thomas closed his eyes tightly, reining in his frustrations that, yet again, the pirate Captain Adams had managed to escape his grasp. It was now a three-year chase, and still, he had never come close to even attempting to board his ship.

His chair creaking as he shifted his weight backward,

Thomas remembered the day he had been given the order to capture and bring back the pirate captain. His career to that point had been one of rising accolades, and he had been given the best ship in the fleet... as well as the warning that the man was a wily one who would likely evade him numerous times. In his arrogance Thomas, however, had ignored those warnings entirely, thinking that he would surely be the one to capture the pirate. His failure was slowly driving him mad.

"Dearest!"

Glancing up, Thomas rose quickly as his mother walked into the room, dressed in her finery.

"What do I owe the pleasure of your company this morning, Mother?" he asked, after greeting her with a kiss on the cheek. "My ship leaves in an hour."

"I have come to say goodbye, of course!" she exclaimed, looking a little disappointed in his reaction.

Thomas narrowed his eyes, knowing his mother had another intention. "And?"

She blinked twice, the pale blue eyes that mirrored his own flicking away from his face. "And I may be accompanied by a friend."

Barely keeping a hold on his temper, Thomas stepped away from his mother and ran a hand through his dark hair in exasperation as he returned to the chair behind his desk.

Marie's eagerness for him to marry had only increased as he aged. Apparently, it would be best if he married, just in case something terribly unfortunate happened to his older brother, who his mother had apparently given up on – for now.

While Daniel would inherit the title of Duke once their father passed away, he had, as of yet, chosen not to marry – nor even spend much time with others.

"I have no wish to meet another young lady who you will

trot out before me like I am buying horseflesh at the auction house," he replied, tersely. "Besides, I have much to prepare before boarding." He lifted his eyes to his mother and saw the frustration on her face.

"Thomas," his mother wheedled. "Do you not wish to have some beautiful young lady waiting for you when you return from the sea?"

"No," he replied, firmly.

"A wife? Children?"

"No, and no," he retorted. "I would not put anyone in that situation, Mother, particularly not children."

She frowned. "What situation is that, Thomas?"

He sighed heavily. "The situation where they might very well be robbed of a husband and father," he replied. "The sea is not always kind."

In his years of working for His Majesty's Navy, Thomas had seen how the sea could claim a life. It was a danger he accepted every time he set foot on a ship, but he had vowed that he would not marry until he had left that life — which did not seem apparent any time in the near future.

To his surprise, his mother did not respond with shock as he had expected. Instead, she simply shook her head at him. "You have chosen a dangerous profession, Thomas."

"No, I have chosen a *respectable* profession, mother," he clarified. "You would not wish me to waste my life now, would you?"

"But there is no need for you to be there!" his mother exclaimed. "You can retire from the sea, Thomas. You already have your fortune and can live as you please. Parties, soirees, cards…society!" Her face took on a rapturous look. "Why you shun that, I shall never understand."

At least there is one thing we can agree on. Thomas had never been attracted to the idea of living with nothing in particular to do. Yes, his father was a duke, and yes, he did have something of a handsome fortune, but that did not mean he intended to waste his life on drink and women. His brother, the heir apparent, might prefer that to any kind of useful endeavor, but it was not for Thomas.

"I'm afraid I must ready myself to board, Mother," he said, rising from his chair and walking over to her. "It has been wonderful to see you. Now if you'll excuse me."

His mother kissed his cheek, her countenance suddenly cold. Thomas shrugged it off, having become well used to her attempts to manipulate his behavior into doing what she wanted.

"Thomas," she said slowly, "it saddens me to see you like this."

"I do not understand you."

"You used to be so… jovial. So free. So interested in all that life has to offer."

"I was naïve."

"Tell me you are still not hunting down this single pirate," she said, with a wave of her hand. "You have not caught him yet?"

"Goodbye, Mother," Thomas replied, refusing to answer her questions. "I shall visit once I return to shore. Please do pass on my regards to Father and the rest of the family."

With a quiet humph, his mother turned on her heel and marched from his office, clearly irritated with his refusal to respond as she wished. Relieved, Thomas sank down into his chair and tipped it back, looking up at the ceiling as if for guidance.

If only his mother could understand the desperation he felt in his inability to, thus far, capture the one man the Navy found so elusive. Many pirates roamed the waters, but the man they called Captain Adams was able to outrun their ships with seemingly great ease. They would hear a report of where he was, only to get there and discover that he and his legendary ship, the *Gunsway*, were gone. He seemed to know when and where they would be coming for him and always managed to evade their grasp.

Thomas had originally laughed to himself over the ineptitude of those who had gone before him in their inability to capture one man. However, that arrogance had faded quickly as, time after time, the man managed to give him the slip. Apparently, he paid his crew so well that none wanted to turn on him. No one was willing to be paid off in order to provide information so, in short, Thomas knew very little about Captain Adams and, in over three years, had only once caught sight of him.

Thomas had joined the Navy out of a desire to explore the world and see beyond the ballrooms of England. He had yearned for the freedom of the seas and ports bordering the oceans. Instead, he was now trapped in a never-ending chase that consumed his every waking moment.

Frustration fired through him as he allowed his chair to fall back down and sat up straight, his square jaw set as he thought about the elusive pirate. The man was mocking him with his seemingly easy escapes. Other captains in His Majesty's Navy ostensibly had no issues in capturing pirates, bringing many to justice, but still, Thomas failed in his task. Shame hung over him like a dark cloud, knowing that many in the Navy found his failure something of a joke.

Thumping his desk, Thomas vowed in his heart that this time, he would find and capture the pirate Adams. His scourge would no longer blight the seas, stealing from whomever he chose and keeping whatever he found. There had to be someone, somewhere, that could help him in his quest. He just had to find him.

"Captain?"

Looking up, Thomas got to his feet as his first mate, Smith, entered the room.

"The ship is ready for you, Captain Harrington."

Nodding, Thomas gathered up his papers and walked around from behind his desk. "Very good. All of my luggage is in the cabin already, I presume?"

Smith nodded, standing aside as Thomas preceded him out of the door. Walking to the docks, Thomas stood and took in his ship. It was one of the Navy's finest, cutting through the heavy seas with ease and giving him peace of mind as he boarded.

"We are to make for Arwenack Castle, Captain?"

Thomas nodded. "Yes. I have received reports that the *Gunsway* has berthed there. It seems Captain Adams has returned to British waters after spending many months away. Perhaps this will be the opportunity we have been seeking."

"I hope so, sir."

The fervency in the first mate's voice matched Thomas' own strength of feeling. The crewmen, he knew, were similarly growing weary from their lack of success, and he feared he was losing their trust.

"Weigh anchor," Thomas instructed, "and let us pray that the wind remains favorable."

Whether Captain Adams was in the port of Arwenack Castle remained to be seen, but he fully intended to make it a worthwhile trip regardless. Someone there must have seen the pirate, and from that, he might be able to make a proper sketch of him.

Then he would make up a paper, offering a generous reward for Captain Adams, and would instruct his crew to plaster them anywhere and everywhere they could find when they came into port. Thomas couldn't fail again. Adams would be in his custody soon – by any means necessary.

CHAPTER 3

"*P*apa," Eleanor hissed, as she pulled the cloak's hood a little more tightly around her face. "We must be quick."

"Hush, child," he replied, calmly. "None of His Majesty's ships are in the vicinity. We can take some time here. I have gifts to distribute."

Eleanor trudged alongside her father, silently fighting the tingling at the back of her neck, telling her to hasten back to shore as promptly as they could. She never felt truly safe on dry land, fully aware that they were always at much greater risk of capture. Her father had always been wanted by the Navy, but for the past three years a certain Captain Harrington had come closer than they would have liked. The fact that they had managed to evade him thus far did nothing to calm her troubled mind. She wished her father would give his gifts to the poor more hastily than he was doing, but he insisted on talking to each person they met. He wanted to encourage them, she supposed, finding that she could not fault him for that.

It had taken many weeks to return to England from the

Caribbean, their holds almost bursting with treasure. They had stopped to store much of it safely away, in a place only she and her father knew, but the rest had been given to the crew and now to the poorest in society. It was not that they did not trust their crew, but her father had always taught her that it was best to have some secrets, that not everyone was completely trustworthy. In the dead of night, she had boarded one of the smaller boats, her father in the other, and together they had rowed over an hour until they reached the mouth of the caves.

It had been there that Eleanor and her father had stored their treasure, in one of the caves that lay far away from the shoreline, through twists and turns of the canal. How her father had discovered such a place, Eleanor did not know, but she had felt relief flood through her – as it always did when they rounded the last bend – when she saw that all of their past prizes were still there.

That was their fourth trip to the cave, and still Eleanor was not quite sure she would know the way herself. Her father would give her the map to it one day, he promised her, but until then, the exact location was hidden in his mind only.

The crew had been overjoyed to receive their pay and such a hefty bonus. While the first mate and one or two of the cabin hands remained on board, keeping the ship out of sight of the port, the rest of the crew had taken the boats to shore and were currently enjoying themselves with all manner of entertainments. Eleanor guessed there would be some muddled heads in the morning, but that was to be expected after so long at sea. Her father had never been so inclined – at least, since she had travelled the sea with him – but he had always taught her the importance of a satisfied crew.

Her father was now bending down to speak to a man who

appeared more dead than the alive. His skin was paper white, his bones practically sticking through it. He pointed to one of his legs, shaking his head. Her father's face filled with compassion, and he handed a small bag to the man, who took it with a puzzled frown. That frown changed to astonishment and then to tears as he looked inside.

Her father then hailed a hackney, helped the old man up into it, and shouted instructions to the driver. The old man kept a hold of her father's hand for as long as he could, before finally having to let it go as the hackney drove away.

"Where did you send him, Papa?" Eleanor asked, wandering over to him. "He looked as though he were about to draw his last breath!"

"That man is only as old as I am," her father replied, slowly. "His leg is deformed and no one cares enough to help him. I have sent him to my friend's house with enough money to support himself for some time."

"You have a friend here?" Eleanor asked, confused.

Her father laughed, pulling his hood up again. "I have many friends throughout England," he replied. "They know of my desire to help those less fortunate. So long as the people I send have the funds to care for themselves, they will not be turned away."

Eleanor shook her head. "You are the most generous man, Papa." In truth, the prize on her father's head angered her, for there were far worse men to chase. Yes, she knew pirates were thought to burn and pillage — and to be fair, there were many who filled the stereotype — but her father was not that kind of man. He shared his wealth, giving it to those who needed it the most and, more than likely, saved them from squalor and ultimately, death. He was everything she aspired to be, and even though she was of an age to forge her own life, her father still had a great deal to teach her.

A sudden gust of wind blew a piece of parchment drifting

along the road in her direction. She snorted when she saw it, holding it between her thumb and finger as though it were rubbish. "The Navy is still seeking pirates." There was nothing specific about Captain Adams or the *Gunsway*, but still, it reminded Eleanor of the dangers on land.

"Harrington will not stop until he has caught me," her father replied mildly, taking the parchment from her and throwing it over his shoulder. "You need not concern yourself with him though, Eleanor. He is easy enough to predict."

That was more than true. Those who worked for the British Royal Navy were all of the same ilk and had all the same training. Their moves were predictable, their boats easy to spot on the horizon. They didn't have the same command of their ships the way her father did. True, there were fewer pirates as the years went on, but the sea didn't seem to respond to the naval fleet in the same way it did for those who lived with it. It hadn't been too difficult to evade capture, although there had been one or two close calls with Harrington. It was the closest the Navy had ever come to Captain Adams, and as flippant as her father was about it, it worried Eleanor.

"One more visit and then we can return to the boat," her father smiled, walking up a small alleyway and knocking on a door. Eleanor followed behind, peering into the old houses, which looked as though one gentle push would knock them all over. This truly was one of the poorest areas in the port.

"Adams!"

Eleanor followed her father just as he stepped inside, welcomed in by an older man with white, wispy hair and a grizzly beard. Eleanor stood in the doorway, listening as her father laughed with his friend, before handing over some more of his treasure. Smiling to herself, Eleanor heard the man exclaim over the gift, his voice growing hoarse with emotion.

It wasn't too long before her father came out again, bidding his friend farewell. Eleanor bobbed her head and smiled, realizing that the man in the doorway only had one leg.

"He was one of your crew, wasn't he?" she asked as they walked swiftly toward the shore.

Her father grinned at her. "Nothing gets past you, my girl."

"What happened?"

He lifted his shoulders. "Cannon fire. Ripped right through the ship and his leg. For a long time, I didn't think he would survive but he's one tough fighter. Kept going until he was back on his feet. Well, on his foot, I should say." Chuckling, Captain Adams shook his head. "Jones was always a faithful crew hand. He worked hard and fought hard. I swore I'd look after him, no matter what happened."

"And now you do," Eleanor murmured, filled with admiration. "Your loyalty to him does you credit, Papa."

"Jones was loyal to me, so why should I not take care of him merely because he can no longer sail?" her father asked. "Loyalty should always be rewarded. Remember that, Eleanor."

Eleanor didn't reply, but simply smiled and walked on in silence. Their lives were not based upon the gold or the other treasure they found, but rather compassion, kindness and a sense of justice as well as expecting unshaken devotion from their crew. Eleanor knew of no other crew as loyal to their captain as her father's. They would not find a better captain. Captain Adams treated his crew fairly, although punishment was always meted out when necessary. He paid them well, kept them from the Navy, and guided the ship through the waters with ease. Eleanor hoped that one day she might be able to mimic her father in everything.

Eleanor's feet crunched on the sand when they reached

their small rowing boat, but as her hand grasped the carved wood, the small hairs on the back of her neck stood up in warning.

"Papa," she said, softly, "something's amiss."

He nodded, his mouth set in a grim line. "I feel it too. Keep a watchful eye, Eleanor."

Climbing into the boat, Eleanor waited as her father pushed it into the waves before he jumped in himself. They rowed hard, keeping the boat quite close to the shore, just in case they would need a place to hide.

"There!" Eleanor exclaimed, pointing as she spotted a Navy ship. Its colors were flying high in the wind, and it was clearly making its way toward the port.

To her surprise, her father grinned at her. "They won't find us, Eleanor. The ship is too well hidden."

"But the crew," she stammered, remembering that most of their crew were probably blazing drunk in the port. "What about—?"

"Don't worry," he reassured her, smiling, slightly irritating her with his ease at danger so nearby. "We'll make the boat ready to sail. No one else knows where we hide the ship now, do they?"

Eleanor shook her head. They'd been coming to the port at Arwenack Castle for almost as long as she could remember, and no one had ever found the *Gunsway*. Her father had discovered a deep, dark cave in the cliff face, tall enough and wide enough to hold at least three ships. They couldn't risk taking the rowing boats to shore, and the crew would have to swim a few lengths to reach the safety of the ship once again, but they were well accustomed to it. The jagged rocks on the shore prevented anyone from walking into the caves, and, so long as no one from the Navy spotted their small rowing boat, they would be quite safe. The only hazard was if they were found from the ocean, as then there would be nowhere to run.

"What shall we do?" Eleanor asked, anxiously. "We cannot just sit out here."

"Row," her father laughed, pulling on the oars as hard as he could. "They have not yet rounded the cliffs. Even their best spyglass will not be able to spot us from that angle. Once they reach the port, that is a different matter, so you must row hard, Eleanor."

She didn't bother to reply, saving her energy. Pulling hard on the oars, Eleanor worked her muscles until there was barely any breath left in her body. Their boat soon began to cut through the water, making its way swiftly toward the *Gunsway*. They arrived at the caves just as the Navy ship reached the port.

CHAPTER 4

*E*leanor barely slept that night, too busy worrying about the Navy ship in the port. It was just too close for comfort. Her father, on the other hand, set Morgan and the two remaining crew the task of readying the ship to leave and then proceeded to fall fast asleep.

Thankfully, the news that the Navy had arrived in the port had spread through Arwenack Castle almost at once, and most of their crew returned to the ship before any of the sailors reached land. There were a few stragglers, of course – the ones too drunk to swim. She kept an anxious watch until, finally, the last man climbed back on board, just as the first fingers of dawn appeared on the horizon.

Captain Adams shouted orders and, within a few minutes, the *Gunsway* left the safety of the cave and began to sail away from Arwenack Castle and Captain Harrington.

"We found this, Captain," said one of the men, pulling off his cap to reveal a piece of parchment. "Looks like they're trying to pin you down for good this time."

Eleanor peered over her father's shoulder, gasping at the face that stared back at her. Someone had given the Navy a description of her father, and now his face was plastered over posters seeking his arrest. It wasn't a perfect likeness, but it was close enough that her father could certainly be identified by it. On top of that, the Navy had substantially increased the reward for her father's capture. It did not seem to bother Captain Adams in the slightest, although Eleanor could not say the same for herself. Her stomach tightened as she read the words, anger slowly growing in her chest toward Captain Harrington's unceasing chase.

"Why is he so hell bent on arresting you?" she exclaimed. "It's been three years since he started this mission, and he still hasn't given up."

"I'm a pirate, Eleanor, in case you had forgotten," her father replied jovially, slapping her lightly on the back. "The Navy wants us all taken from the sea. For some reason, they believe these waters belong to them!" he snorted disdainfully. "We'll just have to keep proving him wrong. And I find the more you evade them, the more they want you."

"You've escaped him again, Captain!" the crewman grinned, as Captain Adams tore the parchment to shreds and threw it into the wind. "Where are we headed?"

Captain Adams considered for a moment, before grinning. "Back to the Caribbean, I think. We have enough supplies?" he turned to Eleanor, who nodded. The first mate had organized all that when they had gone ashore.

"Then let's pray for favorable winds to take us far from here," Captain Adams replied.

"And more treasure to fill our holds." Eleanor smiled, her tension slowly dissipating as they sailed farther and farther away from Arwenack Castle. Her father had repeatedly escaped Captain Harrington for the last three years. She didn't need to worry. The man would never catch up to them.

* * *

THOMAS GRITTED HIS TEETH, reining in his temper. "What do you mean, they're not here? We were told with complete certainty that they would be ashore."

His commander shook his head. "I'm sorry, Captain."

Dismissing the man, Thomas fought the urge to walk into the local tavern and drink until he forgot all about Captain Adams. He'd never been a man to overly imbibe – until the past year, when despair from his fruitless quest began to overwhelm him and it was the only way he could forget for a time.

He had been so sure that they'd finally catch up with the pirate captain this time, only to be proven wrong once more. Thomas' hopes had begun to fade like the sinking of a ship the moment they had come into port and the *Gunsway* was nowhere to be seen. Of course, the locals had refused to breathe a word about the pirate or his crew to the Navy, all except for one man who had been so drunk he'd not cared about what came out of his mouth. He gave them a good description despite his state, which meant they'd been able to have a few posters drawn and distributed on the very same night — but still, not a word had been said about the pirates' whereabouts. Apparently, Captain Adams was very well liked around these parts, with folk finding him "generous and kind," which Thomas could not bring himself to believe. Most likely, the man brought fear and terror to the people of Arwenack Castle, threatening them not to say a word about him. If they did, then who knew what the man might do? He was a pirate, after all.

"What am I to do now?" he asked himself, his jaw clenching as he considered his options. None came to mind. If he boarded the ship once more and began to sail, to where would he even chart his course? The *Gunsway* could be anywhere by now, with no clue as to where it was headed. If Captain Adams knew that the Navy was still on his trail, then Thomas figured he would put as much distance between himself and them. Perhaps back to the Caribbean?

Frustrated, Thomas walked smartly back toward his ship, finding the waiting crew prepared for his next orders.

"Sir," the Lieutenant saluted, standing straight and waiting for Thomas to speak.

Clearing his throat, Thomas nodded to Lieutenant Taylor. "Tell me your opinion, Lieutenant. Where do pirate ships tend to congregate? Particularly when one wishes to hide from His Majesty's Navy?"

The Lieutenant looked surprised, then thoughtful. "There are a great many places, Captain, but I would suggest that the *Gunsway* might seek warmer waters."

"It's as I thought as well, to the Caribbean. Whereabouts would they go?"

The Lieutenant thought for a moment, although a slightly uneasy expression came over his face. "Likely Port Royal, if I had to hazard a guess. They've been known to stop there before to trade, particularly after a decent haul. That is a long voyage, however, Captain. What if they remain nearby? We would waste weeks."

Thomas sighed inwardly. He hated that the Lieutenant was right, but what was he to do? He had asked the man to speak plainly, and his point was valid. What if they traveled to the warmer waters of the Caribbean only to discover that the *Gunsway* had not voyaged there in some time? Would he be playing right into Captain Adams' hands?

"Do we have the supplies for such a voyage?"

The Lieutenant gave a crisp nod. "We could be ready to weigh anchor in a few hours."

Making a decision, Thomas nodded his agreement. "Then do that. We sail for Port Royal."

* * *

PORT ROYAL WAS A DISGUSTING, filth-ridden place. Thomas wrinkled his nose as he marched through the town, thankful that the British were, at least, trying to better it. Ascending the steps into the naval post, he nodded to the waiting commander before climbing to the outlook point.

The top of the post gave him an excellent vantage point from which to study the seas. They had been in Port Royal for two days thus far and, as yet, had not seen any sign of the *Gunsway*, nor of Captain Adams. He cursed under his breath. Their destination had been a mere guess as to where the pirate might go next, and now here he was, searching desperately for a ship that he did not know for certain was heading in this direction.

Captain Adams could be anywhere.

Thomas' gaze landed on Gallows Point, where the bodies of the latest two pirates hung, gently swaying in the warm breeze. It was somewhat ghastly, but a reminder of the penalty for piracy. He was a part of this, a part of the British Royal Navy that was attempting to bring some kind of order to this pirate-ridden land.

However, Thomas knew that the pirates still ran Port Royal in many ways. As much as the British liked to think they were in charge, it was the pirates who ran the establishments and the trade. They were the economy here and the residents were not inclined to turn on them. Port Royal was large and the Navy simply had not sent enough men to deal with all those who arrived here. On top of that, he was not always able to tell, just by appearances, which men were pirates and which were not. Thomas also had to admit that, as dirty as this place was, the people were good spirited and seemed to enjoy their lives.

Closing his eyes for a moment, Thomas tried to tell himself that the trip was not entirely wasted. He was seeing the world, was he not? And at least here, they could display Captain Adams' reward, in the faint hope that there might be someone desperate enough to lead them to his whereabouts.

"I need a drink," he muttered to himself, placing his hat firmly back on his head and walking back down below. The tavern was not the cleanest, but it was certainly the best on this side of Port Royal. Carefully picking his way through the muck on the cobbled streets, Thomas pushed open the door, found a dark corner, and took a seat in the scarred wooden chair.

"Captain Harrington," the barman said, coming over to him, wiping down the surface in front of him with a cloth as dirty as the table itself. "Can I get you a drink, sir?"

"Whisky," Thomas murmured quietly.

He placed his hat on his knees and shrugged out of his jacket, wanting some solitude for the time being. He did not wish to be disturbed by all manner of sailors, some whom might come seeking entrance into the Navy's command post, others who were only there to mock him. Nodding to the barman, he accepted a whisky with a mutter of thanks, before staring into it as if it would provide the answers to all of his problems.

Three years. It had been three years since the chase had begun.

Thomas threw back some of the amber liquid and let it burn down his throat and into his chest. Was this what his life was going to become now? Sailing from port to port, all in search of one man? Was there not more for him to explore?

Thomas had always had a desire for adventure, a desire to

escape his small world and live in a much bigger one. He did not want to simply do the usual thing of marrying, producing some children and then settling down to a life of liquor, gambling, and mistresses. No, there was more to life than that, and Thomas had been keen to explore it.

The Navy had provided that opportunity for him, and yet, Thomas' world had slowly shrunk as he'd been forced to focus all of his resources on one man. At times, he envied the pirate captain, although he would never admit it to anyone. To be a pirate meant freedom. Freedom from living under orders, from doing what you were told to do. A pirate captain, unlike a naval captain, had full command of his ships and of the seas. Pirates could travel anywhere they wished, do anything they wanted, all without constraint — with the exception of avoiding ships like his. Of course, the values Thomas so upheld rebelled entirely against such a life of theft and deceit. He could not, however, resist the temptation to dream of the wonderful freedom they had.

Perhaps he could buy his own ship, hire his own crew. Whilst his family was wealthy, Thomas knew such a route would bring repercussions. For one, he would never find a respectable marriage when the time came. He would be seen as something of a vagabond. Then there was always the question of his continued funding, for, of course, he would have to pay his crew and buy enough supplies to keep the ship going.

Eventually, Thomas would either have to find some kind of treasure — which he had no knowledge of how or where to begin — or simply steal or fight for wealth. He'd be no better than the very pirate he chased.

He drank the rest of his whisky before slamming the glass back down on the table, calling for another. He was stuck, completely embedded in the Royal Navy with no way out. He could return home, of course, but that would take him back into a life he truly despised. No, for the time being, he would have to simply continue his chase of Captain Adams and wish that, when he finally caught him, it would not only spell the man's demise, but also lead Thomas to freedom. That was all he had to hope for.

CHAPTER 5

"I'd say he looks quite miserable," Eleanor whispered, clenching her fists in her skirts, "and I am glad of it."

"We should return to the ship," the first mate warned. "It is some miles away and, now that we know he is here, your father will wish to weigh anchor immediately."

Eleanor knew he was right. Their trip to Port Royal had been a successful one, bartering for more goods and ensuring that they had enough food for their next adventure, but it was always intertwined with danger. Now that the British were attempting to "clean up" Port Royal, they had been forced to be much more careful. However, the port was large and the *Gunsway* had been anchored a few miles off shore with flags lowered so that they could not be easily identified. Besides that, they were only one of many ships near Port Royal, and, as soon as it began to grow dark, Eleanor knew her father intended to leave and return to open water.

She and Morgan were securing the final goods in town and had stopped at the tavern. It was there that Morgan had pointed out Captain Harrington sitting at the bar, alone. Eleanor knew the best course of action was to leave as soon as possible to warn her father, but she couldn't help but be intrigued. His name had hung over her head for three years now, yet she had never seen him herself.

Now, watching him sit there, morose and alone, he seemed just an ordinary man. One who, at the moment, seemed defeated. Perhaps... perhaps this wasn't a risk, but an opportunity.

"I'm going to speak to him," she said, standing abruptly.

"No, Adams," hissed the first mate, referring to her as he had always done, "you cannot."

Eleanor frowned. "Why not? I am in skirts, am I not?" In truth, she much preferred breeches, but she drew too much attention when she wore her usual garb on shore. It was better that, on this particular visit, they stay hidden. "He will believe me to work here." In one capacity or another.

"Why would you speak to him?" Morgan whispered, hoarsely. "There is no need, Adams. We already know who he is!"

"Because I wish to look him in the eye," Eleanor replied, fiercely. "I would stare into the face of my enemy, unafraid." She paused, losing her ire as practicality reigned. "Besides that, he appears to be in his cups and may have some worthwhile information for us. I will meet you back at the ship."

Eleanor's rank on the ship was an undefined one. The crew respected her and considered her one of their own. Her father had made known his intentions for her to succeed him one day, but at the moment, she held no type of rank at all. She didn't give orders, but she also did not follow every order given by the first mate — at least, not in decisions off the ship. Without giving him a chance to argue, she pushed away from the table and walked over to the barman, requesting another whisky for Captain Harrington.

"You're with him, are you?" the barman grunted, looking her up and down as though she were one of the easy women who worked around Port Royal. She wished she could invoke the Adams name, but the fewer people who knew her identity here, the better. "Well, at least you're cleaner than the other ones who come here."

Eleanor bit back her harsh retort, managing a hard smile as the barman handed her the whisky. Picking it up, she walked over to the captain, her heartbeat increasing as it did when a battle loomed as she approached him.

"Did I hear the barman say you are a captain?" she asked smoothly, sitting down opposite him without invitation.

A pair of eyes the color of shallow waters looked up at her warily. "I did not think His Majesty's Navy was much admired in these parts."

Eleanor pretended to be upset and pouted. "I was merely bringing you another whisky, sir," she replied quietly, lowering her eyelids. "I am sorry if that was the wrong thing to do. You simply look a little unhappy. I thought I might change that."

The hard expression dimmed as he raised his eyebrows at her and, to Eleanor's shock and dismay, she realized that he was quite a handsome man. She told herself the surge of attraction to him was nothing more than a physical urge as she kept the smile on her face while he sat back and studied her with those cool blue eyes framed by chiseled cheekbones.

His jaw tightened as his eyes wandered over from her face, over her shoulders upon which her hair hung loose, down her figure, pausing where she knew her breasts were swelling over the neckline of her blouse, though not as suggestively as most of the barmaids. His countenance changed, and he smiled at her, surprising her with his crooked grin, a dimple etched into one cheek.

He ran a hand through his straight dark hair as it fell

from its tie, and her fingers itched to run through its silkiness. She clenched them into fists.

This is your enemy, Eleanor, she reminded herself, *you feel nothing but hatred.*

"I should not have been so harsh," he murmured, reaching for what was now his fifth whisky, at least by her count since she had begun watching him. "My temper quite gets the better of me at times, particularly in days of late. Now tell me, what has brought a woman as beautiful as you to a place like this?"

"The same thing that brings us all here in one way or another," she replied with a coy smile of her own. "Pirate treasure."

He chuckled ruefully, shaking his head. "Most of it is said to be gone. The glory days of the pirates are over. If you are seeking out those clinging to the days of old, why choose this table, then? You must know an officer of the Royal Navy is not the place to find your treasure."

"You looked so lost over here by yourself," she replied, with what she hoped was a look of pity. "I thought you could use another drink — and some company."

"Your presence is welcome," he replied, leaning in and twirling a lock of her hair around his index finger. "I must admit, I am rather lonely."

Eleanor said nothing, the rising hairs at the back of her neck warning her that this had been as bad of an idea as Morgan had warned her. She had to leave—now. If she stayed, she would have no choice but to follow through on this charade she had begun.

"Excuse me, sir," she said, getting up from the table as gracefully as she could. "There are other customers."

His hand shot out and strong, calloused fingers wrapped around hers, keeping her close. "The barman will not mind, I am sure," he said, firmly. Eleanor saw him lift his head and catch the barman's eye, who, to her horror, simply chuckled and tipped his head toward one of the doors to his left.

This was all going disastrously wrong. A surge of fire swept through Eleanor as she forced herself to sit back down. She must behave as any other woman might, not the woman she truly was. The woman she was playing to be would be eager to accept the captain's attention.

"Can I get you another whisky, sir?" she asked, hoping that this might be a way to make her escape.

"No, I think not," Harrington murmured, throwing back the remains of his glass before trying to stand. He swayed slightly, as even a man of his size had knocked back quite a few glasses in a short space of time. "I have not enjoyed a woman's company for a long while now. I am not normally a man who pays for a good time, but there's a spark to you – you speak to me. Perhaps you're just what I need to clear my head and lift my spirits."

Eleanor felt her stomach tighten as he wrapped a strong arm around her waist and led her away from the table. She turned around looking for Morgan, but he had disappeared, likely to finish their business of the day. She was no innocent young woman, but this was her *enemy*, the man who wanted to see her father hanged. She had to be smart. If she ran now, he would only become far too suspicious, and if he followed her, she would be putting her father and the crew at far greater risk than they would have been from the start. Why had she not listened to Morgan and left the man alone?

The worst part of it all was that Eleanor had to admit to herself that she was not completely opposed to the idea of going to bed with this man. Strong muscles revealed themselves through his shirt, and his drunken clumsiness was lending somewhat of a charm to his bearing. She felt like a traitor as her body and mind struggled over how to respond to the British captain.

"Top of the stairs to your left," the barman grinned, as Harrington slammed down some money on top of the bar. "Thank you, sir. Most generous."

He's paying for my services, Eleanor realized, going cold all over. She tried to breathe slowly as he stumbled up the stairs, her mind working furiously. Maybe she would be able to knock him out somehow, and then make her escape.

"What is it that you need relief from, sir?" she asked, hating that her voice trembled a little. "Perhaps I can help you in other ways."

He snorted, pushing the door open slightly too hard so that it banged loudly against the next wall. "Unless you can find Captain Adams, my dear girl, then I do not think you can relieve my true torment."

"Ah, so you are hunting a pirate," she trilled, leaning in and running a hand down his chest as though she was comforting him. "If he is causing you so much difficulty, then why do you not simply give up? I am sure the Navy will find much better things for you to do. After all, he is only one pirate and there are so many around Port Royal. You could take your pick."

Throwing his hat and coat onto the chair in the corner of the room, the captain faced her, his face ravaged. The change in his demeanor shocked her, although she kept her features schooled into a sympathetic smile.

"I dream of freedom," he rasped, stepping closer and grasping her arms with strong hands, as if willing her to feel his desperation. "I can have none until I catch him. The Royal Navy does not accept failure."

"Must you stay in the Navy?" she asked, reaching a hand and running it over his hair as she had yearned to do earlier. "Have you no other options?"

"Not if I am to keep my family from dishonor."

"Leaving the Navy would cause this?"

"They were shocked when I joined the Navy. Now I have spent three years in a search of one man. I am a laughing-stock, but if I find him, bring him to justice — well then, perhaps, I will have restored the honor I lost and can find a new path."

Eleanor looked up into his eyes, finding them cold but haunted — and in that moment, something shifted within her. "You're trapped."

"Trapped," he nodded, as if musing over the word, "that is exactly what I am."

"Despite travelling the world over the open seas."

"I'd prefer to see the world on my own terms," he replied, a faraway look in his eye. "However, I have seen more than I would have ever thought possible. Even this town, as dirty as it is, has beaches that are something to behold, and the palm trees and crystal-blue ocean are simply... magnificent."

"No, I do not suppose they have beaches such as these where you are from," she replied with a smile, thinking of the rocky caves where they stored their treasure. "Where will you go next?"

"I'll follow the pirate until the day I catch up to him. I should hope that day comes sooner rather than later." Tipping his head, his eyes blazed into hers as he ran his hands lightly down her arms, catching her hands. He uncon-sciously stroked her wrists, sending tingles through her body. "Over and over I search for him, and always come up short."

"Perhaps you are not meant to capture this particular pirate," she murmured, which stilled the stroke of his fingers.

"Why this sudden care for Captain Adams?" he asked, eyeing her warily from somewhat glassy eyes. "Do you know the man?"

She let out what she hoped was a carefree laugh.

"The fabled pirate Captain Adams? I could only wish. As

I'm sure you know, Captain, he does not frequent such establishments as this. I'm afraid you will have to continue your
search for Captain Adams — and your freedom —
elsewhere."

"That I will. In the meantime, perhaps you can help me
remember what freedom tastes like."

Eleanor shivered as his mouth descended, catching his
kiss and finding that she didn't shrink from it. His lips were
hard and firm, but she refused to allow him dominance,
kissing him back with as much passion as she could muster.

Stop, came the voice in her head, but its insistence that
this man was her enemy was slowly being drowned out by
the need that was pulsing through her from where he
stroked her back with his strong fingers, to the way he was
tasting her, ravaging her mouth like she never would have
imagined a naval man ever could.

She couldn't think straight. His fingers were already
tugging at her bodice, clearly desperate to reveal her body
underneath. It wouldn't be the first time Eleanor had been
with a man, although it had been some time since the last. It
wasn't a frequent occurrence. While she and her father were
both pirates, she was still his daughter and as far as he was
aware, no one had ever touched her, so she had been
discreet.

Eleanor couldn't help her gasp as his hands found her
buckled skirt, undoing it quickly. He slipped his tongue
between her lips to battle with hers, his hands running over
the curve of her hips.

There was nowhere to go. Nowhere to run. She was
pressed back against the wall of the small room, knowing
that if she made any attempt to leave, he might come after
her and eventually discover her father's whereabouts. If she
remained, then she would have to play the part of a working
girl and wait until he fell asleep, as they always did. And,

deep down, she wanted this. Her soul would never submit to it if she didn't.

The shirt fell from her shoulders, her skin now bare to him. The lace ties of her undergarments fell prey to his eager hands and soon Eleanor found herself entirely divested of her garments, while he remained completely clothed.

Stepping back, he ran his eyes over her, a slow grin spreading across his face.

"Perfect," he murmured, moving back in front of her again and boldly caressing her breasts. "You're just lovely. Perhaps my fortunes have turned and you're the good luck charm I've been looking for."

"You are still clothed, sir," she murmured, closing her eyes as his mouth sought hers again. "If you wish to make this quick, then may I suggest that—"

She did not have time to finish her sentence, for he broke the kiss for a moment so that he could throw his shirt over his head. The rest of his clothes were easily discarded until Eleanor felt warm skin pressing against her own.

Her breath caught as his lips moved from her mouth down her jaw and to the curve of her throat, his hands kneading her breasts. Heat burst through her veins as he continued his exploration of her body, leaving her trembling with unspent need.

"You are a warm one, that is for sure," he muttered, slowly lowering his head farther so that he might catch one of her nipples between his teeth. Eleanor could not help the moan that escaped from within, betraying her need for him. He chuckled low in his throat, before scooping her up in his arms and depositing her on the bed.

His intrusion into her body was immediate, shocking her, but she was more than ready for him. Eleanor lifted her hips to him as he began to move, lengthening his strokes. Her body, which had tightened upon his first entry, began to slowly relax as she became used to his presence, only to grow hotter with the fire he was building in her.

Eleanor was sure that he was only interested in his own pleasure, but she could not stop the desire growing in her own body. His hands continued to caress her curves, roving over her with reckless abandon. Looking up into his eyes, she saw the spark of heat in them and heard his breath coming more and more quickly. He was reaching his peak, but she did not intend to allow him to do so without finding her own release.

Boldly, she grasped his hand and pressed it to her center, crying out at the slightest of touches. Astonishment stopped his movement for a mere second before a wicked smile came over his face and he pressed his thumb against her, circling his thumb over her. His movements were not finessed, but Eleanor did not care. Arching her back, she closed her eyes and lost herself entirely, only aware of the growing tension that drew her ever closer to the brink.

He moved faster now, groaning as he neared the edge of his release. Eleanor met him there, her body practically coming off the bed as she convulsed around him. Stars exploded in her vision, blood thundering through her veins.

He lifted himself off of her and shouted aloud as he found his release, his seed dampening the bed beside her. Then he collapsed forward, still breathing hard.

"I was right — I do feel much better," he said, his eyes already beginning to close. He absently stroked her hair as he slowly drifted off to sleep. "I needed that — you. Needed you. I paid the barman for your services."

She slowly got up from the bed. She had slept with the enemy — and enjoyed it. Dressing as quickly as she could, Eleanor tried to push away the shame that crept into her soul, unable to look at him as she hastily left the bedchamber.

What had she done?

CHAPTER 6

*H*urrying toward the shore as though she was being chased – by inner demons if nothing else – Eleanor saw her father ahead of her, turning toward the beach, and she lifted her skirts and ran to catch up with him.

"Papa, we must leave at once," she said urgently once she reached him.

He nodded, his face grim, before motioning to the men ahead of them. "Yes, Morgan has already told me of Captain Harrington's presence. Can't say I'm pleased that you took it upon yourself to speak with him."

Eleanor prayed that her father would never find out that she had done so much more than speak with him. "I had to find out what he knew."

"And did you?" Her father eyed her with a tight jaw as they crossed the sandy beach toward the small boats that would carry them back to the *Gunsway*.

Her throat spasmed and she had to clear it before speaking. "Yes, I did, Papa."

Snorting, he shook his head, grasped her hand, and

helped her into the boat. "Hurry now, Eleanor. We must make haste."

Eleanor grasped one of the oars, while three more of the crew took the others. As they rowed, the boat began to cut through the water, moving quickly away from Port Royal.

Eleanor closed her eyes, although that certainly didn't erase the image of herself with Captain Harrington. Perhaps it had been too long since she was with a man, but to give herself to the one man who was intent on capturing her father was utterly shameful. Her body filled with heat once more, although it was for more reasons than the guilt that filled her when she looked at her father – it was also the memory of how it had felt to be with the captain, how, if it wasn't for what his life's goal was, she would welcome his touch again.

"You do not need to worry, Eleanor," came her father's voice, cutting into her thoughts and making her jump. "We will be away before nightfall. The captain will not even know we were here until it is too late."

She managed a tremulous smile. "Just as always."

He chuckled, his face lit with good humor. "Precisely."

Suddenly his smile faded, replaced with surprise as his face grew as pale as if a spirit had risen from the depths in front of them. Eleanor might not have noticed had he not been sitting right next to her, but she heard the hitch in his breath, saw his hand slowly climb up his chest.

"Papa?" Eleanor gasped, dropping her oar and reaching for him, panicking when he didn't immediately answer her. "Papa!"

"I'm well," he gasped, his words hoarse and weak as he waved his hand in front of her, "just some pain."

Eleanor grasped his free hand, studying him, wishing his normal jubilance would return, but a thick ball of worry tumbling about in her stomach told her that this was not to be ignored. His face had now a pale sheen of gray, his hand still scrabbling at the collar of his shirt.

"Hurry!" she cried to the crew on the boat, still holding onto her father's hand as they looked on anxiously. "The captain is sick!" As they responded in earnest at the urgency in her voice and the love of their captain, Eleanor realized the most she could do for her father now was to row as hard as she could along with them, and she grabbed her oar and gave it all the muscle she had.

She kept glancing over at him, and, thankfully, by the time they reached the *Gunsway*, her father's color was slowly beginning to return to normal as his pain ebbed away.

"I am sure I must have had one too many mugs of ale," he joked, although Eleanor could see the line of concern on his face. "To my cabin, I think."

Eleanor could tell his strength was waning, noting his slight stumble as he walked. She kept close to his side, wrapping her hand around his arm in an attempt to support him. Whatever ailment had befallen her father, it may have receded, but had taken with it his strength.

"I just need to rest, Eleanor," he said, quietly. "You can run the ship until I awaken, can't you?"

"Of course I can," she replied firmly, hoping that the crew would simply accept her command without question. "Are you sure you are not in any more pain, Papa?"

He sat down heavily on his bunk, pressing her hand with his. "I feel no more pain, Eleanor, I promise. I just need to sleep, perhaps, for I am quite worn out." His smile fell a little flat. "Hearing Captain Harrington was at Port Royal did surprise me, I must say. Some days, Eleanor, I am just weary from being on the run."

"Then we shall go to open water for a time," she said, firmly, "or perhaps near the Iron Caves? That way we can go ashore if we need to."

Patting her hand, he held out his hat before leaning over until he was lying flat on his bunk. His eyes began to close almost immediately. "You decide, Eleanor," he murmured, apparently already too tired to stay awake for even a moment longer. His breathing grew heavy as he drifted into sleep, leaving her worried for his health and anxious over her new role.

Walking outside onto the deck, she glanced at the first mate, who gave her a barely perceptible nod. Apparently, he was willing to listen and take commands from her, which bolstered her courage.

"The captain is unwell," she stated, trying to keep her voice firm. "He has appointed me to take command until he is recovered."

She paused for a brief moment but didn't catch a single word of dissent. She waited for a hint of argument, but instead, each of the crew simply looked up at her, a few nodding, all waiting for her to tell them what they should do next.

"We will set sail for the Iron Caves," she continued, looking around. "Are all the crew returned?"

"All but three," the first mate replied. "I can see them approaching now."

Eleanor nodded. "Very good. The moment they are on board, we are to weigh anchor. The Royal Navy is on the other side of the island, and we cannot risk them knowing our position. Understood?"

"Aye, Adams — Captain Adams," Morgan replied, giving her a small smile before turning around and shouting orders to the crew.

Eleanor stood in front of the ship's wheel for a few minutes, watching the crew scurry about the deck, making ready to depart. Hope filled her. She could do this. She could command the crew and take them out to the open water for safety. All she had to do was keep the ship — and herself — away from Captain Harrington.

* * *

ONE HOUR LATER, the *Gunsway* was already making its way out to sea, with all of the crew safely on board.

"Captain!"

Eleanor took a breath, waiting for her father to respond.

"Captain Adams!"

The shout came again, louder this time, making her start with surprise. In a rush, she realized the man was speaking to her, seeking to get her attention.

"Yes?"

Flushing, she hoped the crew hand hadn't noticed her slip and lifted her chin just a notch. The last thing she needed was to lose the respect of the crew.

"Captain, it seems there be a ship on the horizon."

"A ship?"

He nodded, as another crew hand handed her the spyglass.

Eleanor lifted it and closed one eye as she looked across the churning water. The clouds were already gathering, and the darkness was slowly creeping in. Sooner or later, they were going to have to drop anchor, but Eleanor wanted to get as far away from Port Royal as possible. Port Royal. A place she would never think of again without the memory of her time with Captain Harrington. She wished she hadn't known who he was, she considered, before her eyes landed on the ship on the horizon.

Her stomach dropped.

"The *Savage Soul*. It's heading straight for us," she said, softly, lifting the spyglass to try and identify the flags, just to confirm her suspicions. "How did they know we were here?"

Handing the spyglass to the crew hand, she turned to the first mate as he joined them.

"Probably just bad luck, Captain," Morgan replied. "We've been fighting with the *Savage Soul* for many years, but they just keep coming back," he grinned. "Probably because we've got the best crew around and we always get the most booty, better than any other pirate ship on the seas!"

"That may be true, but now isn't the time to test them," Eleanor replied, tersely. "How should we avoid them?"

Silence covered the crew for a brief moment before the first mate nodded to dismiss them. Stepping a little closer to Eleanor, Morgan looked at her with gravity in his eyes.

"You be the captain for now, Adams."

Drawing in one long breath, Eleanor slowly realized what it was he was trying to say. Asking others what to do was showing her uncertainty, her weakness. She should be the one shouting orders at them. Closing her eyes briefly, Eleanor fought against the urge to rush into her father's cabin and waken him to seek his direction. Now was the time to prove she was worthy of the faith he had in her. She had to take on the mantle of responsibility and that meant deciding for herself what was best to do. The crew was looking to her to make the choice: head toward the ship and fight, or take action to remove themselves from their path.

Eleanor swallowed. "We will avoid them. The *Savage Soul* is looking for a fight, but we're not going to give them one if we can help it. Not right now." She remembered with absolute clarity the last time they had met. The *Savage Soul's* Captain Wayland was a man of little mercy. He took joy in his killings, and she'd heard it said that the head was the last thing he'd remove from a man, ensuring his captives suffered the greatest amount of pain before they finally passed. A shudder ran through her. Her father had always ensured that the *Gunsway* was prepared for a fight with the *Savage Soul*, although he tried not to seek one out. That is what she must do now.

"We will keep course for the Iron Caves as we try to outrun them," Eleanor said, her voice firmer as she stepped into her role with certainty. "But prepare the crew and the ship for battle in case." Drawing in a deep breath, she set her jaw. "I will take the helm."

The first mate grinned but dipped his head. "Very good, Captain."

Eleanor turned on her heel and marched back into her father's cabin, her intention clear. This night could easily turn deadly, and she had to be ready to take on whatever it was that came to them.

Walking to her father's side, she looked down at him with fear in her heart. He looked so pale, with deep shadows under his eyes. He was always so strong, so courageous, yet he seemed to have aged years in just hours. She brushed the hair from his temple, but he did not stir. She might think he was gone from this world if it was not for the slow rise and fall of his chest. His skin was cold and clammy, and she tugged another blanket up over him.

Please do not leave me, Father, she begged, silently. *I need you still. The crew needs you. You've fought so many battles. Fight this one more.*

Stepping back, Eleanor forced herself to leave her father sleeping, before turning to find his hat. Picking it up, she brushed her cheek gently against the dark feathers that adorned the brim, then inhaled, taking comfort in the scent of salt and the sea emanating from the black leather. How long her father had worn this, she couldn't remember, but she was sure it had been a great many years. The hat had become synonymous with his name. Steeling her resolve, she placed it on her own head, aware that it was far too large but knowing that it would be a visual reminder to the crew that she was in the captain's place for as long as it took for her father to regain his strength. It would also show that she was more than willing to take on the role. She could not forget to respond to the call of "Captain" again.

"I will do my best, Father," she promised, touching his hand. "I will send someone in to sit with you. Return to us soon."

Stepping back outside, she shouted at one crew hand, and then another, directing them just as her father would do. There was a momentary pause before the crew hands began to scurry across the deck, with one entering her father's cabin as she'd ordered.

Eleanor was, for the time being, Captain of the *Gunsway*. Now she'd better act like she deserved the title.

CHAPTER 7

*T*homas rolled onto his side with a groan, his head already beginning to throb. He didn't know how long he'd slept for, but he did know he'd drunk far too much whisky. He had never been much of a drinker in the past, but lately he'd been using it to numb his frustrations. That and the tavern girl he'd taken to his bed. A woman who should have been nothing more than a quick bit of fun, but who he couldn't seem to get out of his mind.

Flopping back onto the pillow, Thomas threw a hand over his eyes and allowed a slight smile to play over his lips. The girl had been beautiful, warm and welcoming, and he'd taken his pleasure quickly. He was surprised that she'd been so responsive, remembering how she'd clung to him as her own crescendo had peaked. Thomas hadn't exactly taken such women to bed often, leaving these activities to his crew. There had been something about this one, though, that had spoken to him and stripped away his usual hesitation. He would have to slip out of the tavern as quietly and as quickly as he could – even as he knew he never should have left his ship. At least it was in good hands with his first mate.

Dressing with haste and ignoring the pounding in his head, Thomas couldn't help but remember the beauty of the woman he had taken to bed. Her flaxen hair had spread out across the bed sheet, her green eyes burning with an inner fire as he'd touched her. Perhaps, if they stayed for a time, he might come to her again, provided the barman could be discreet.

Marching down the stairs and back into the tavern, he cringed inwardly as the barman gave him a ribald wink.

"Making your way back to the post now, sir?"

"I am," Thomas replied, firmly. "I have paid you, I believe?"

"More than enough," the barman grinned. "You're always welcome back here, Captain."

Thomas cleared his throat. "Thank you." Stepping closer, he realized that he did not even know the young woman's name. "I would be interested in spending more time with that particular girl on my next visit to Port Royal," he said, in low tones. "Might you ensure she remains available to me?"

A flicker of confusion crossed the barman's face. "She ain't my wench, sir."

"What do you mean?" Thomas asked, his frown deepening. "I thought she worked here."

The barman shook his head. "I believed her to be with you, sir. I can keep an eye out for her, of course, but that's all."

Thomas nodded and pushed away from the bar, his mind filled with questions, but he dared not speak them aloud. This was neither the time nor place, and he would not embarrass himself any further by asking the barman more. Muttering his thanks, he placed his hat firmly on his head and marched out of the tavern.

Walking toward the naval post, aware of the late hour, Thomas remembered something about Captain Adams being mentioned with the woman, but could not quite recall what it was he said.

Frustrated with his lack of clarity, he marched into the naval post, determined to push the woman from his thoughts. He had greater things to focus on.

"Captain, sir!"

Halted almost the moment he walked onto the post, Thomas removed his hat and directed his gaze to the man seeking his attention. "Yes, Hayes?"

"We've been waiting for your return, sir. It appears that the *Gunsway* was seen making its way out of port on the other side of the island."

Hope sparked to life at once, finally pushing away thoughts about the girl who had warmed his bed. "What? When?"

"About two hours ago, sir," came the reply.

"Two hours?" His hands curled into fists as he regarded Hayes. "Why was I not told?"

Hayes glanced away. "We have been searching for you, sir..." he murmured, trailing off as though he did not quite want to accuse the captain of being absent without any explanation as to where he was going.

Thomas didn't need the man to say it, however, for he was hard enough on himself. If he missed the *Gunsway* now, it would be entirely on his own head.

"Captain!"

Another man rushed into the office, his eyes wide. Thomas turned to him, his brows lifting at the midshipman.

"Captain, the *Savage Soul* has been spotted on the horizon."

Thomas' heart jumped in his chest. "The *Savage Soul*? You are sure?" He was aware of the gathering darkness, wondering how the man could have seen the ship so clearly.

"Yes, sir," the midshipman replied, trying to recover his

breath. "I was out on patrol, and we were about to make our way back in toward shore when one of the men spotted the ship. The sun was sinking below the horizon, but there was enough light to make out their colors." He swallowed, his lips thinning. "It was the *Savage Soul*, Captain."

Nodding, Thomas placed his hat back on his head, preparing to depart. "And are they coming into port?" He was sure they were not, for it was more than likely that the lookout on the *Savage Soul* would have spotted the patrol boat.

The midshipman shook his head. "They turned, sir. They looked to be heading in the direction of the Iron Caves."

"Prepare the ship," Thomas replied firmly. "We set sail at once."

The midshipman hesitated. "Sir, there are clouds rolling in."

"If the *Savage Soul* and *Gunsway* can sail, then we surely can as well," Thomas retorted, striding from the room. "Ready the ship, and someone find the crew!"

Storming out of the office, he made for his ship, thunder pouring through his veins. The clouds were rolling in, which meant that it would be difficult to sail. There could be a great many dangers, hidden from view, but Thomas refused to dwell on it. He was going to sail after the *Savage Soul*, and he would bring at least one pirate to justice.

Then, he would set his sights on Captain Adams once again. Thomas grimly grinned into the darkness. He knew that the *Savage Soul* and the *Gunsway* were the worst of enemies. He had heard the rumors about the long-held animosity between the two pirate ships, which bent in his favor. If the *Savage Soul* was in the same vicinity as the *Gunsway*, then chances were they might be preparing for a fight. If he could get in the midst of it, then his prospects of catching both pirate captains increased significantly. Or perhaps they would just take one another out first.

His brow furrowed as he tried to decide his best option. Sailing into the middle of two battling pirate ships also meant danger to his crew and his ship. Pirates were not predictable folk. Both ships could turn on him and attack as one.

"We'll decide once we catch them," he muttered to himself as he boarded the ship, thinking this was too great an opportunity to miss. "First we must get them in our sights."

* * *

THE CLOUDS CONTINUED to pour in as the ship moved into the deeper waters. Thomas stood at the helm, his grip tightening on the rope as the waves began to buffet the ship. His resolve remained steady. He was determined to return with at least one pirate in his brig.

"Can you see anything?" he asked, tersely.

The cadet shook his head. "The clouds are thick and we must move slowly, Captain."

Thomas gritted his teeth. "What of the pirate ship?"

The Lieutenant, Taylor, drew closer, dismissing the cadet. "Captain, I must be honest. You are risking both ship and crew by continuing with this course. There are submerged rocks and sand banks all around Port Royal, and we are barely able to see where we are headed as it is. Our ship is larger than the pirates, we cannot follow the same course. The clouds are so thick that I fear soon we will be unable to see our hands in front of our faces."

"What is it you would wish me to do, Lieutenant?" Thomas shouted into the wind, letting loose with his frustrations. "The *Savage Soul* and perhaps even the *Gunsway* are within our reach!"

The Lieutenant maintained his steady gaze. "Begging your pardon for speaking so boldly, sir, but you won't have a ship to reach them with if you continue with this reckless course."

Thomas seethed, wishing he could ignore the Lieutenant completely and just continue as he'd planned, but he had to heed Taylor's words. He knew that this was already a dangerous course, but now the chances of losing the ship were growing significantly. If he was to ground the ship, then some of the crew could even lose their lives. Letting out a groan of frustration, Thomas closed his eyes and attempted to rein in his anger.

"Very well," he said, harshly. "Drop the anchor. We will remain here until morning."

"Yes, sir," the lieutenant said, turning around and swiftly barking orders to the rest of the crew. Thomas could almost feel the tension that surrounded the ship suddenly break as his change in orders was relayed.

"If it relieves your frustrations any, I do believe that the *Savage Soul* will not be able to make any headway either, Captain," Taylor added, standing smartly to the side of the ship. "Most likely, they will drop anchor as we have done. They will not risk their ship."

Perhaps, Thomas thought, although the pirates knew these waters so much more intimately, that they had much better sense of where was safe to sail. Letting out a long breath, Thomas shot Taylor a look. "I apologize for my obvious irritation, Lieutenant."

"It is understandable, sir," Taylor replied, unflinching. "Captain Adams and his pirate crew have evaded us for many years. Do not think you are the only one who is desperate to capture him once and for all."

Walking to his cabin, Thomas saw how the skies had turned, making it impossible to see one end of the ship from the other. The lieutenant had been quite right to push for them to drop the anchor. It had been foolhardy to consider a pursuit in this weather.

Shutting the door, Thomas threw off his hat and shrugged out of his coat. Yet again he had thought he was close to catching the pirate captain, and yet again he had been thwarted. It appeared even nature was against him! All he could do was hope that the pirate ship had been forced to drop anchor as they had. When the first fingers of dawn hit the skies, he would be in pursuit once more, provided the clouds had cleared.

As Thomas lay down and closed his eyes, sleep eluded him, his mind travelling back to the woman, her image refusing to fade. How had a beauty like her ended up in such a position? Her green eyes had initially been filled with ice, but, as he'd kissed her, they'd warmed to emerald pools. Her kisses had become more passionate, her fluttering touches bolder.

What mystery surrounded her! He had no idea of her name, nor of where she had truly come from. If she was not a wench working in the tavern, then what in heaven's name had she been doing? And why could he not let her go, consider her just a pleasurable memory instead?

Thomas forced himself to push thoughts of her away. He would need a clear mind come the morrow, and could not allow it to be filled with thoughts of a woman with green eyes and sunshine-kissed hair. He had a pirate to catch.

CHAPTER 8

"They are still on our tail, Captain."

Eleanor's gut tightened as she lifted the spyglass to her eye. The dark clouds that surrounded Port Royal had not yet reached them out here on the open sea, but Eleanor knew it would not be long before they did so. As she watched, the *Savage Soul* emerged from the clouds, the lanterns on their deck clearly visible in the growing darkness.

"What are we to do, Captain?"

Lifting her chin, Eleanor drew in a long breath. She was not going to keep running, nor hide like a coward. Instead, she was going to make a stand.

"We fight," she said, quietly. Despite being raised on a pirate ship, she was not violent by nature, and yet, this was the best option. It's also what her father would choose. "There is no other way to evade them and I will not spend the next few days and weeks running from them. That is no display of courage."

To her surprise, the first mate grinned. "Very good, Captain."

Eleanor merely nodded, walking closer and shouting her orders. "All hands hoay! Batten down the hatches and prepare to blow the *Savage Soul* down!"

An eruption of cheers met her words as the men began to run across the ship, preparing the cannons and ensuring it was ready to meet the *Savage Soul*. Eleanor knew that their cannons had a longer range than the other ship's, which gave them something of an advantage. The sound of splintering wood resounded in her mind as she remembered the last time there had been such a battle. They had been badly battered but had still come out the victor. It had taken weeks to repair the ship – weeks that they did not have, not with the Navy after them.

She needed a plan.

Striding back to her quarters, she picked up her cutlass and slung it through her belt. She would fight with her crew, defending her father and his ship with every breath she had in her.

"They be closing in, Captain!"

The first mate's shout had her rushing back to the helm, grasping the wheel as she could see for herself without the need for a spyglass that the *Savage Soul* had not slowed.

"Are they in range of our cannons?" she asked.

"Not yet, Captain."

Grasping the spyglass from him, she studied the approaching ship. An idea began to form.

"Prepare the cannons with a bar and chain shot."

"What be you thinking, Captain?" Morgan asked, after shouting the orders.

Eleanor handed him the spyglass before hauling on the wheel, turning them broadside. "We must be in position. When they begin to turn broadside to have us in range of their cannons, begin firing. We must damage their sails and rigging with the bar and chain. Then they will be dead in the water."

"They won't be able to continue turning," the first mate finished, his eyes widening as he realized the extent of her plan, "they will be at our mercy."

Eleanor nodded, her mouth set in a firm line. "And I have no intention of allowing Captain Wayland any kind of freedom," she bit out, "he is mine."

* * *

"Fire!"

Eleanor was nearly breathless as she screamed one order after another. Her plan had worked out just as she'd intended, and the *Savage Soul* was already floundering in the water. The bar and chains she had fired at them had damaged their sails and rigging to the point that they were unable to turn their ship in the water and get the *Gunsway* in range of their own cannons. Eleanor could see men already climbing the rigging in an attempt to fix it, and she ordered her crew to push their own ship closer to the *Savage Soul*.

She swallowed, hard. Should they board the boat? Or leave them in reach of those in Port Royal? If she did that, then the *Savage Soul's* crew members were bound to face the noose. They may be rivals, but that didn't mean she enjoyed seeing men hanged to death for piracy.

She set her mouth in a firm line as she made her decision. She would give them the opportunity for mercy – if they elected to join her crew. She would first ensure that they knew exactly what would be expected of them in return for their loyalty. At least then they could choose to make their escape.

"Do we board, Captain?"

Thinking hard, Eleanor shook her head. "No, we will not." Turning to one of her crew, she pointed to him. "Davy. Take a message to the *Savage Soul*. They are to either join us or we will leave them to His Majesty's Navy at Port Royal, who I'm sure will be along within minutes of sunrise." Nerves clawed at her. "We must be hasty, do you understand?"

"Right away, Captain!"

Within minutes, a small boat was lowered from the *Gunsway*, filled with four men. The rest of her crew were ordered to ensure their safe passage, and, having armed themselves, remained on deck. It did not take more than a few shots for the men on the *Savage Soul* to realize what was expected. It was part of the unspoken pirate's code – one which Eleanor knew many would scoff at, but it was necessary to their way of life. Negotiating with their very lives was not something anyone should ignore.

Eleanor held her breath, twisting her fingers together as the boat reached the *Savage Soul*. The moon shone down brightly on the waters, giving her enough light to see by, but one glance toward the dark clouds at Port Royal told her that they did not have long. The moment those clouds reached them, it would be nigh onto impossible to sail anywhere.

"Do you think we can trust them, Captain?" the first mate asked, as they saw the small boats of the *Savage Soul* being lowered. "It looks like they mean to accept your offer."

Eleanor's eyes darkened, her hand moving to rest on the handle of her cutlass. "No, we don't. After all, they are pirates." She gave him a grim smile. "Captain Wayland, whatever his intentions or hopes, will be shut in the brig the moment he comes aboard."

Morgan nodded.

"And tell our crew to remain vigilant," she finished, slowly drawing her cutlass out as the crew from the *Savage Soul* neared the *Gunsway*. "This could all be a trap."

* * *

THE MOMENT the final crew hand from the *Savage Soul* stood on the deck, Eleanor knew her instincts had been correct. Their captain wore a relaxed smile, one which caused her spine to turn steel with tension. Her men had removed weapons from the crew of the opposing ship, but she knew there would be some hidden out of sight, in boots or pant legs.

"Where is Captain Adams?" Captain Wayland asked, sweeping off his hat in an elaborate bow. "I must thank him for his kindness."

Eleanor lifted her chin, not taken in by the man's attempt to appear jovial, or his willingness to surrender his ship. "You are to be locked in the brig," she replied, tersely, refusing to answer his question. She nodded to Morgan, who moved forward — only for her entire deck to explode with action.

The *Savage Soul* crew ran, as one, at the crew from the *Gunsway*, all of whom fired immediately. Unfortunately, their guns were not particularly accurate at such close range, and soon the sound of clanging swords echoed across the water as the *Savage Soul* crew had taken their advantage of surprise and lifted swords and cutlasses off her men as they fired their guns.

Eleanor did not hesitate. Swinging her cutlass, she joined the fray, fighting for her ship and her father's name.

One young *Savage Soul* crew hand leapt, catlike, from the helm directly in front of her, waving his curved blade in figure eights multiple times. Eleanor cracked a smile, completely unintimidated. The man clearly thought she was untrained in battle, but he was about to suffer the consequences of his foolishness. For a brief moment, she saw uncertainty in her opponent's eyes, immediately grateful for the advantage.

Advancing forward, Eleanor held her cutlass steady, waiting for her opponent to make a move. As she had expected, the man charged at her with his curved blade upheld, going to his forward swing and following it with a back swing. Eleanor dodged the first and met the second with her cutlass, throwing her entire body weight behind her attack. It pushed his blade back, although she had not quite managed to knock it free of his hands.

Her opponent recovered quicker than she expected. His arcing shot sliced through her shirt close to her belly, the tip of his sword only just missing her flesh as she stumbled back across the deck. Without a second to spare, Eleanor swung her cutlass, attempting to pierce the man's skin but missed by a fraction of an inch. She could see the smirk on her opponent's face, apparently believing that she was going to go down in a matter of minutes. Anger ate through her, filling her with a white-hot rage.

This was her ship.

This was her crew.

She had offered kindness, but had been met with attack. She had been naive. She was trying to emulate her father, but instead had made a decision that could cost her the ship, or at the very least, the respect of her crew. This attack was not entirely unexpected, but she absolutely would not allow such an act to go unpunished. She was not about to stand here and lose the *Gunsway*. She had made a poor decision, one which she was sure all would attribute to her womanhood, and now had to prove her mettle.

With a yell, she pushed forward, swinging quickly with her cutlass. Shouts and cheers from all around her let her know that her crew were doing well, overcoming the attack from the *Savage Soul*.

Striking upwards, her first two strokes were met with an easy defense by her opponent, causing her to change her step, bend at the knee, and strike forward. The cutlass ate through her opponent as easily as air and, as she withdrew her sword, he fell to his knees, looking at her with tortured eyes.

Eleanor did not have time to wait for his death, turning on her heel and preparing to fight once more.

"Playing captain, I see."

Captain Wayland stood in front of her, a gun pointed directly at her chest. A slow grin crossed his face as he lifted one eyebrow.

"An imposter, are you?" he regarded her carefully, tilting up the brim of her hat with his other hand. "Ah, I see now. The daughter." His smile widened. "And a beautiful one at that. Perhaps I might take my pleasure with you before you die."

"I am no imposter," she said fiercely, sweat beading on her forehead at the thought of his threat. "And you will not win this fight." Glancing to her left, she saw her crew was rounding up the rest of the *Savage Soul* men, with some of the dead already being thrown into the water.

"As you can see, *Captain*," she continued, mockery in her voice. "You have no status here. Your ship will be lost to the British Navy at Port Royal – for I do not want such a burden -- and your crew is under my control." She grinned at him, her heart lifting in triumph. "Now why don't you step back, before I feed you to the fishes?"

His smile fell from his face as her crew slowly circled them, ensuring there was no place else for him to go. He waved his gun menacingly, the only threat he had left.

"Then I may as well remove you from your newfound

position, captain," he sneered. "At least then I can rest in the brig knowing that I have finally defeated my enemy."

As the sound of a gunshot rang out, time slowed as Eleanor stiffened, closing her eyes, waiting for death to take her, wondering how much pain she would feel, how disappointed her father would be — but instead, she felt only the wind tossing her hair behind her shoulders.

A sudden thud caused her eyes to open, only to see Captain Wayland lying on the deck, blood pooling around him.

"What?" she gasped, looking around. "How?"

"Eleanor."

Looking up, she saw her father clutching the rail, his face white in the moonlight. He clutched a smoking gun, which dropped to the deck with a clatter as he fell on his knees.

"Father!" she cried, running as fast as she could to him, managing to catch him just as he collapsed entirely. "Father, no!"

"You are captain now," he breathed, his eyes fluttering as he could barely hold his head up. "The crew stands with you."

Eleanor turned to glance at the assembled crew, all of whom nodded as one as they removed their caps from their heads, showing respect to her as well as her father.

"You are brave and bold and strong, Eleanor," her father whispered, his hand tightening on hers. "You are the best daughter a pirate could have asked for. Or any man, for that matter." He struggled for breath.

Moisture splashed on Eleanor's cheek as the skies opened up and the rain that had threatened came pouring down. Thunder cracked and lightning streaked across the clouds, but she paid no heed.

His voice became breathy, as he slowly faded away. "I will see you again, daughter."

"No!" A scream left Eleanor's throat as her father's hand

fell, limp, to the deck, followed by the rest of his body. Tears poured down her face but were washed away by the storm's deluge as she bent over him, placing her head on his chest but feeling no breath, no movement.

He was gone.

CHAPTER 9

*E*leanor was numb, unmoving but for her hair and clothing that stirred in the ocean's breeze. She barely registered the salty ocean water slap at her face as she stood at the rail, her eyes on her father's body wrapped in cloths.

Someone in the crew spoke a few words, but Eleanor couldn't summon the strength to utter a single sound. Her heart was torn.

It had been two days since her father had passed. Upon his death, she had forced her grief deep within, nearly choking on it as she continued with her command of the ship. It had been unthinkably difficult, but she had no other choice as the new captain of the *Gunsway*.

The body of Captain Wayland had been thrown, unceremoniously, into Davy Jones' locker, and his remaining crew was threatened with much the same fate if they so much as attempted to escape. She had not wanted to show them even the slightest bit of kindness, but had known it was what her father would have wished her to do.

She had sent a boat of her own crew to plunder the *Savage Soul*, where they found a fine host of treasure.

The *Savage Soul* crew hands had been given a choice: remain and serve on the *Gunsway*, or be returned to the *Savage Soul* where they might attempt to make their escape from the Royal Navy, torn sails and all. She had not been in the least surprised when the first mate of the *Savage Soul* had taken the option of returning, along with two other sailors. She had merely nodded, and the men had been forced to walk the plank to swim back.

They had cried out in protest, apparently believing that she was going to grant them the privilege of using the smaller boats, but she had remained steadfast. She made them swear to her that they would never reveal her identity, or she would come after them and hang them herself. She respected their desire to remain with their ship, and had been forced to acknowledge that there had been something of a relief in her heart when she had seen the three men begin to swim back toward the wreckage of the *Savage Soul.*

They would have been picked up by the Royal Navy by now – she was sure of it. Not that it mattered. She was consumed by the loss of her father, his body wrapped up tightly and ready to hit the waves in burial. She had sewn him into his hammock herself, weeping as she did so. The privacy had allowed her some time to grieve in peace, pressing his cold hand between hers for the last time.

"May he rest in peace," she murmured now, seeing the crew waiting for her, and she nodded jerkily at Morgan. She watched, tears blurring her vision, as the body dropped from the side of the ship into the waves, landing with a great splash. Guns were fired in salute, as the bell rang out in his memory.

Eleanor blinked furiously, putting the captain's hat firmly

back on her head. Her time for mourning was over, and she must now speak to the men.

"You have accepted me as captain. I am grateful for that. To the world, for the time being, I will remain Captain Adams — the Captain Adams they have known for so long. Not all will accept me as you have."

A murmur of agreement ran through her loyal crew, although the newcomers still regarded her with suspicion.

"When we are out at sea, I will be as I am now," she said, dressed in her shirt and breeches but with her long locks flowing in the wind. "But should we come across another ship, or even when we dock at the port, I will disguise myself as a man. That way I can keep our reputation as the strongest, most powerful pirate ship that ever sailed across these waters intact."

All eyes turned to her, and she saw her first mate nod in approval. She knew that the idea of having a woman in charge was difficult for many of the pirates, but she was going to prove to the world that she could captain a ship — and captain it well.

"Should I hear that any of you have spoken of my true identity, I will make sure that your feet meet the plank," she warned, her voice dropping, "except the weights in your pockets will make it impossible to go anywhere but below the waves." The crew grew silent once again. "I demand loyalty, just as my father did. Anyone who crosses me will be chased across the seas until their life is brought to an end by my hand." Eleanor knew she had to captain with a strong hand, ensuring her power remained intact. She would do what she had to. "Stay loyal to me and you will be paid well. I have no desire to lower any of the standards my father set. A devoted crew is worth more than any treasure we can find. Although," she continued, managing to smile just a little, "we have more than enough of that already."

The crew murmured again, but this time the tone had lightened.

"Now, we toast to Captain Adams," she finished, nodding to Morgan, who began to hand out the liquor she had set aside. "We will drop anchor and spend the remainder of the evening and the night in this place. Remember Captain Adams. The best and bravest of us all." She lifted her glass high, hearing the sailors repeat her words back to her, before draining her glass. Then, turning on her heel, she marched back into her father's cabin — which she would now call her own.

The brandy burned down her throat and into her chest, helping her keep her resolve until the door shut behind her. It was only then that she gave in to her emotions and allowed herself to sag against the wood behind her.

The strength she had summoned ebbed from her body as she wondered if she would ever accept the loss of her father. He had been the only family she'd ever had, and now he was gone. It was quite true that some of the crew members were like family to her as well, but blood ties were different. Tears began to drip from her eyes down onto her cheeks as she placed her hat on the writing desk by the large window, seating herself in the chair beside it. Looking out across the sea through the small window, she saw the sun begin to sink low in the sky. It would soon hit the horizon, turning the sea red and gold. It was always a beautiful sight to behold, but Eleanor's heart was too heavy with grief and pain to appreciate it today.

She would captain as her father had, being both strong and generous. Her father's kindness to the poor was something she would continue, helping those who had no means to support themselves.

She would do her father proud. Of that, she was certain.

* * *

Thomas folded his arms over his chest and smiled smugly at the three pirates now being frog-marched into the prison cells. They had said very little, but one had told him that Captain Wayland was now at the bottom of the ocean, killed by Captain Adams.

Unfortunately for him, the *Gunsway* was beyond his reach – for today, anyway. The clouds had cleared just as dawn had broken, and when he had seen the wreck of the ship bobbing in the water, his initial elation had ebbed somewhat when he had realized it was not the *Gunsway*. Still eager to catch a pirate, he had urged his crew to reach the wreckage of the *Savage Soul* as quickly as they could.

He had to confess some disappointment at finding only three pirates on board. They had been attempting to put some kind of raft together in order to make their escape to Port Royal. Had he captured Captain Wayland, then that might have been some consolation, but to discover that Captain Adams had killed the man simply brought him more frustration.

"And you have no idea where the *Gunsway* might be?" he asked again, as the men were locked in. "I promise you that if you tell me something, then it will be better for you. I can ensure you do not swing from the gallows."

One of the men stepped forward, his face pressed against the bars. "And you are asking me to trust your word on that, are you?"

Thomas was affronted, glaring at the pirate now. "I am a Captain in His Majesty's Navy, not some lowly pirate that lies and cheats and steals his way across this world. Of course my word can be trusted!"

"Then let's have your word on parchment," the pirate replied, still sneering. "Prove to me that you'll let us keep our lives and then, perhaps, we might tell you something about where the *Gunsway* might be going."

"They killed your captain!" Thomas replied, hotly. "Why do you not just give them up?"

In response, the pirate simply spat at Thomas' feet, muttering something about "the code" as he went to sit down in the corner of the cell.

Thomas had to restrain himself from marching into the cell and grabbing the man by the throat until he gave up the location of the *Gunsway*, but he knew that was not the way to discover what he sought. His fists clenched as he walked away before he took an action he regretted. The pirates' mocking laughter followed his steps as he made his way back outside, heat climbing up his neck and into his cheeks.

"They're not giving anything up then, sir?" Taylor, waiting for him, asked.

"They want my word on parchment first that they'll not swing."

Taylor snorted indelicately. "Most likely they won't be able to read a word you've written. Are you going to do it?"

Thomas sighed, staring out at the horizon. "If we want to catch the *Gunsway*, then yes, I'm going to have to. Have the clerk write up a contract at once. I want the ship readied within the hour. We set sail again as soon as we have an idea of their location."

The Lieutenant nodded and walked away, leaving Thomas alone. For a brief moment, he wondered how far this task would take them from Port Royal, if he would have a chance to return and seek out the mysterious woman who had laced herself into his thoughts. He shook his head, banishing her image. He had to stay focused on the task at hand, not become distracted by thoughts of *her*. It had been a quick tumble, that was all. So why had she so entranced him?

"Sir!"

The clerk interrupted his musings, holding out a parchment for him.

"That was swift," Thomas said, pulling his thoughts from his daydreams and focusing on the paper he held. "You have done well."

"I know how important this is to you, sir," the man replied, bowing slightly. "I wish you luck in finding Captain Adams. I am sure he will be in your custody soon."

Thomas grimaced. "One can only hope," he muttered, before striding back toward the cells. He had a pirate to catch.

CHAPTER 10

TWO MONTHS LATER

*E*leanor sat quietly, looking over the maps on her father's table. She supposed it was hers now, but she wasn't sure if she would ever become used to the change.

Following the battle with the *Savage Soul,* they had traded the treasure they had gathered for gold, and stopped at the ports where her father had frequently dispensed of his riches to the poor. There had been a few minor skirmishes along the way, and while there had never been any risk to her experienced crew, she had proven herself as much of a leader as her father ever was. She still felt she had so much to learn, but she had earned the crew's respect and loyalty, and that was what mattered most.

A few days away from Port Royal, she had called for the anchor to be thrown down. Morgan helped her fill the boat, and she proceeded into the caves she and her father had always traveled to deposit the riches. The map had always resided solely in her father's head, yet somehow she had navigated the twists and turns of the complicated route they took. It amazed her how much her memory had held, and soon enough she came upon their stores with equal parts relief and elation.

She had considered taking Morgan with her, but in the end had decided against it. As loyal as he was, it was too much temptation to give to a member of the crew. As she rowed through the dark, wet cave walls, she had come to the realization that she would have to make a choice. Like her father had with her, she had to share the secret with someone, or should something happen to her, the gold and jewels hidden deep within the cave would be lost to them forever. Someday, someone would find it, but it would be of no use to the people who could benefit from it now. It reminded her of how alone she truly was.

They had now been sailing uninterrupted for a week, finally making for the Iron Caves where they might rest. The islands were along the route at nearly equal distance between Port Royal and England. Her father had kept a stockpile at their island destination, so there would be enough food and rum to keep the crew contented for many a day. It would also give her time to finally come to terms with her father's death and to decide upon their next course of action.

"Captain!"

The first mate's voice was urgent.

"Yes?"

"There's a ship bearing down on us. A mighty fine one, too."

Her heart dropped. Just when she had let down her guard.

"Any idea of its identity?"

"Looks like the Royal Navy."

She sprang to life at once, calling to the crew to man their stations as she pulled on her father's coat and wrapped a cloth around her face so that only her eyes were showing. It was a poor disguise, but it would have to do. Marching out onto the deck, she caught sight of the ship advancing toward them at great speed — causing panic and fire to combine and roil about within her stomach.

As much as she loved the *Gunsway*, she knew that they could not outrun the Navy ship, not when it was already advancing on them. The wind was not particularly favorable, and their cannons were out of range of the Navy vessel. How had they found them? Had someone given up the location of the Iron Caves?

"What are you thinking, Captain?" Morgan asked, with anxiety in his voice. "They will be almost upon us soon!"

Eleanor brought her thumb and index finger to her forehead, her mind sifting through the various possibilities before her. The most important thing was for her to save her ship and her crew since she knew that Harrington, who was undoubtedly on board the Navy ship, was only after one thing. her. Of course, in truth, he was chasing another Captain Adams, her father, but he wouldn't know he had died. How could she possibly save her ship?

"Assemble the crew," she shouted, her heart pounding in her chest as she stood at the helm. The first mate screamed orders at the crew and soon, everyone stood on the deck looking up at her.

"Captain Harrington seems to have found us," she said, loudly. "But I will not endanger your lives. He seeks only Captain Adams, and if I were to be in one direction and the *Gunsway* in another, then I know which direction he will go."

"Captain," the first mate replied, his brows furrowing, "you cannot be thinking to hand yourself over!"

"That is precisely what I will do," Eleanor replied, hearing the muttering begin in earnest. "I will not put your lives in danger. Once the Captain realizes he has been outsmarted again, I will find a way to escape." She tried to smile, even though nerves clawed through her belly. "After all, the Navy has not exactly proven itself to be cunning and stealthy now, has it?"

Thankfully, a couple of her crew hands chuckled.

"The ship belongs to you," she continued, turning to Morgan. "I will meet you again at the Iron Caves. Wait for me there."

The crew waited to see what the first mate would do. He studied her for a moment longer, before nodding and then saluting, agreeing to meet her at their proposed destination.

"We will wait for you, Captain Adams, for as long as it takes," he said, loud enough for the rest of the crew to hear. "The *Gunsway* will always belong to you."

Eleanor nodded, then barked a few more orders at the crew, who scurried to do her bidding. Morgan drew closer to speak with her privately, his weathered face lined with concern.

"I have sailed for many years with you and your father," he said, quietly. "Are you sure about this, Eleanor?"

After so much time together on the seas, Eleanor knew his concern for her was true. "I have to save my ship and my crew," she replied earnestly. "Lower one of the boats. I will sail to the east, but the Navy ship will see me almost as soon as I hit the water, I am sure of it. The moment they turn toward me, you must force the *Gunsway* faster than it has ever gone before. I will try to provide enough time that you will not be followed."

"And you will meet us again at the Iron Caves," the first mate finished, clasping her hand in a gesture of friendship. "Be careful, Captain."

Eleanor nodded tersely, pushing the recognizable hat down a little more firmly onto her head and then walking to the side of the *Gunsway*. The boat was lowered into the water and she climbed down after it, trying to ignore the way her hands were shaking with nerves. Soon she would be the captive of the man she had despised for years – and also the man who had taken her to his bed. What would he do once he discovered her true identity? Would he remember her? And, if he did, what would the consequences be for her?

Grasping the oars, Eleanor pushed her boat through the water. Every fiber of her being told her to rush back to the *Gunsway*, to climb aboard and attempt to sail away from the Navy, but she knew it would be futile. If she did not do this, then the crew would end up in the brig, if not left to sink beneath the waves of the very water they called home. The *Gunsway* would be taken by the Navy, or blown to smithereens until it became nothing more than another sunken wreck.

There was no other option. She would find her way back to her ship. There was no doubt in her mind that the *Gunsway* would wait for her by the Iron Caves, for as many days as it took her to return. There were ways to escape the clutches of the enemy. Eleanor's father had taught her well. Soon it would be time for her to put his lessons into practice, helping her to find her way back.

She pulled hard, her muscles beginning to scream as she put everything she had into taking the boat in the opposite direction of the *Gunsway*. She prayed that her plan would work, that the Navy ship would soon spot her and wait for her, giving the *Gunsway* time to make an escape. The pursuing ship loomed closer, and soon shouts began to make their way across the water toward her.

"At least it's working," she muttered to herself, letting the cuffs of her father's coat hide her small hands. She saw a boat being dispatched from the side of the Navy ship and made no attempt to sail away. She would show them what bravery looked like, what loyalty meant. If she could protect her crew and her ship, then that was exactly what she would do.

Within minutes, rough hands grasped at her arms, pulling her bodily from her boat into their own. She tried not to cry out as they bound her arms and her hands, glad that the frilled lace at the cuffs hid her fingers mostly from view.

"Not much meat on you, Captain Adams!" one of the men laughed, sneering at her. "If we feed you to the fishes, they'll not have much of a feast!"

Eleanor kept her mouth shut, relieved that they hadn't pulled down the cloth covering her face. They were probably under order to leave her as she was. Her stomach knotted as she was forced to climb up the side of the ship, struggling to do so with bound hands. Laughs and jeers met her ears as she did so, making her burn with frustration and anger.

"Straight to the brig!" came a loud, clear – familiar – voice, the moment she was pulled onto the deck, "And no one is to go near him but me!"

Eleanor lifted her eyes and looked into the face of Captain Harrington, flushing deeply but glad that her features remained hidden. He had never laid eyes on her father before, so would not be surprised at her lack of height, although his poster had shown a bit more girth. Desperately hoping that no one would push the hat from her head, she allowed herself to be frog-marched down below deck, and into the small, airless cell beneath.

Sinking down heavily onto the bench, Eleanor wrinkled her nose at the smell. She didn't know who had been here before her, but the entire cell stank, the walls wet and the air stale. It was nearly dark, with slivers of sunlight peeking through the boards above her head. It was not unexpected, but she wondered how long she would be down here.

You have to stay calm, Eleanor, she told herself, as the ropes dug into her arms. *Don't speak. Let them discover for themselves who you truly are.* Drawing in a long breath, Eleanor let her nerves slowly dissipate. The *Gunsway* was, by now, making good time away from the Navy ship. In the time it would have taken for her pursuers to reach her and to haul her up on deck, to slow the ship enough to wait for her, the *Gunsway* would have made its escape and was, by now, clean away.

"I will see them again," she muttered to herself under her breath. "Courage, Eleanor."

A door rattled, followed by the sound of heavy footsteps on the stairs. Someone was coming — and Eleanor did not have to guess who it could be. Harrington had made it very clear that it was only he who was to face Captain Adams, so his face at her cell was not unexpected. Eleanor shrank back against the wall of the cell, refusing to lift her head.

"You wear that hat as though it is some kind of trophy," he scoffed, standing tall outside her cell. "You, however, are no longer a captain, unfortunately. It will be the gallows for you."

Eleanor's throat tightened, but she said nothing. She would not let herself think of the gallows, nor the many pirates who had swung on them before. Somehow, she would make her escape. She had the element of surprise, which in itself was an advantage. But how would he react when he discovered that the person underneath the captain's clothes was, in fact, the woman he had already taken to bed? Had he even been lucid enough during their encounter to remember her face?

"You have escaped me for many years," Harrington continued, his voice soft but filled with menace. "But no longer. You think that your crew are safe? Do you truly believe that your sacrifice means that I will stop chasing the *Gunsway*?" He shook his head with a humorless smile. "No. My quest has begun with you, but I will finish it and sink your ship – after I relieve it of all of its treasure."

Swallowing, Eleanor forced her breathing to remain even

as she kept her head bowed, anger simmering in her stomach. How had she ever let anything but hate grow between the two of them? She had to keep her disguise intact for as long as she could, giving the *Gunsway* every moment it could to get away.

"I suppose they will have to seek a new captain, now that you are gone," Captain Harrington continued, almost casual in his tone. "Unless you hope, of course, to somehow escape our clutches and return to them, which, I assure you, is impossible. Every precaution is in place to keep you on this ship."

Silence stretched between them.

"You are not going to speak?" Harrington's voice grew angry, his hands now grasping the cell bars. He had clearly anticipated this moment so long, and now Eleanor refused to give him any response. "You remain mute when your captor speaks to you?" He snorted. "I should have known you would show such little courage."

Balling her hands into fists, Eleanor kept still, even though the urge to defend herself — and defend her father's honor — almost pushed her to the brink.

What she did not expect was for Harrington to push his key into the lock, swinging the cell door open. Strong hands gripped her collar, pulling her to her feet.

"Who do you think you are?" he raged at her, his eyes blazing. "You refuse to speak to me?" He gripped tighter, causing Eleanor's clothing to choke her. "Pirates do not deserve to wear a captain's hat!" Harrington shouted, lifting her up against the side of the ship wall. "This does not belong to you!"

Without warning, he let her go, and she stumbled. He grabbed her hat and threw it to one side. The cloth fell from her face, and Eleanor felt herself entirely exposed. She kept her head down for a moment, until she decided now was the time to show him he hadn't won – not in the way he thought. Lifting her chin, she looked directly into Harrington's face, smiling triumphantly when his mouth and eyes opened in shock.

He released her immediately, stumbling back as she pushed herself away from the wall to stand tall before him.

"*You*," he spluttered, his voice a breathy whisper as recognition flared in his eyes, "you — you are not Captain Adams."

"Captain Adams has escaped you again," Eleanor lied, stepping closer to him. "And it seems you have captured a *woman* in his place." She shook her head at him. "Now, Captain Harrington, just what are you going to do?"

CHAPTER 11

*T*homas was frozen in shock as he stared at the woman before him, dread filling his heart. He finally thought he had caught Captain Adams, but not only had the man escaped him, he had sent a woman in his place. This woman, one he had obviously used before to gather information.

The act was entirely dishonorable, but it had worked well. He had recognized the well-known hat in the rowboat and had let the *Gunsway* go in order to keep the captain, despite understanding his tactic.

That the woman from the tavern, the woman who had haunted his dreams was somehow, inexplicably, in his brig, staring at him defiantly, those eyes he remembered so well gleaming emerald as she triumphantly stared at him, rattled him more than he cared to admit. Thinking of the way he had just handled her poured shame over his entire body.

"What are you doing here?" he rasped, stepping back from her in shock, lifting a hand to rub the back of his neck. "Who are you?"

She pursed her lips and turned her head, refusing to say more.

"I cannot have a woman aboard," he continued, still quite unable to take her in. "The crew will believe that it is terribly bad luck. And if they do find you, well… you'd require protection as you'll be the prettiest face they've seen for some time."

To his surprise, she snorted indelicately. "How interesting, Captain, that the Royal Navy would have such difficulty keeping their hands off of me, while from *pirates* I receive nothing but respect."

He reddened, considering their own encounter. "How could they allow you on board? Are you the woman of one of them?"

"Hardly. I am no one's woman but my own, and am certainly thought no less of because of it. I am welcome on board the *Gunsway* and am as much of a pirate as the rest of them," she said, her head held high as she looked him directly in the eye defiantly. Thomas wasn't sure how to respond, for he wasn't used to women who challenged him so. "Our crew is more gentlemanly than you will ever be."

Thomas scrambled furiously to find something to say but was robbed of speech. He grew hot and cold in turn, realizing that Captain Adams had, indeed, bested him yet again. Had he sent a woman simply to mock him, to place bad luck among his crew? Had she gone willingly? By all appearances, she certainly seemed to have backbone, standing there with eyes that flashed whenever she glanced at him. Was it true, as she said, that she was actually a pirate?

A slow realization dawned.

"Did you come to my bed simply to discover my plans?" he asked hoarsely, his voice growing louder as embarrassment filled him.

She laughed loudly. "You did not think, did you, *sir*, that drink and a woman's arms might loosen your tongue?" She shook her head at him, almost pityingly. "How easy it was to get you talking."

He ground his teeth, hating that he'd assumed she had either been a simple tavern wench or someone who sought to have time with a captain. He had been so foolish. Not only had he talked his naval strategy with her, but he had shared with her some of his innermost thoughts as well. He had underestimated this woman.

"Put your disguise back on," he bit out, desperate to return to the deck where he might clear his head. "I will return for you later." He narrowed his eyes as she arched one eyebrow, a coy smile on her lips, clearly trying to taunt him. "And you need not fear that I will take you again," he finished. "I can assure you that I do not touch pirates."

She tipped her head, her smile still on her face as she set the hat jauntily back on her head. "Oh, but it seems that you do, Captain."

Turning on his heel, he stormed along the dirty floor toward the stairs, desperate to get away from her as her laughter chased him up to the deck. This had all gone so terribly wrong and, as the crew cheered him once again, lead settled in his stomach. He had not captured Captain Adams at all. He had been outplayed, once again.

THOMAS POURED himself another drink as the ship lurched through the waves. Frustrated beyond measure, he threw it back in one gulp, letting it burn down his throat and flood his veins. His crew thought he had succeeded in capturing Captain Adams, and he had not the heart to correct them. It was just as well he had forbidden the crew to speak to the pirate, allowing only the cook's boy to go below deck to hand the "captain" some rations.

He could not allow her to remain there, even if she was part of the *Gunsway* crew. A woman aboard would throw his crew into disarray, terrified at the bad luck she would bring to the ship. It was mere superstition, of course, but he could not allow his crew to know of her presence. If they did find her, he liked to think she would be safe but there was no telling. There was only one thing for it: she would have to come to his cabin.

Sighing, Thomas thumped the glass back onto his table. He hated the sight of her, hated the mocking smile she'd worn on her face since the moment he'd realized the truth. Now he was going to be forced to endure her company until they made port. Then, perhaps, he could work out what to do with her. Female pirates were rare, which meant he was at a loss as to how he would be expected to handle her capture. He couldn't very well let her hang. Perhaps he might take the ship out with a skeleton crew and put her ashore somewhere. Maybe an island, where she would not be able to escape.

Letting out a loud groan, Thomas closed his eyes and slid his arms across the table, resting his forehead on them. Once he took the woman to his cabin, his crew would realize an empty cell remained, and the hunt for Captain Adams would resume.

"I cannot keep searching for him," he groaned, knowing that he simply would not be able to face the crew and tell them that Captain Adams had bested them once again. He wanted out, or at the very least a different assignment, even though that would be admitting defeat. He would be the most disrespected, out of all the captaincy, simply because he could not catch one pirate.

Lifting the liquor bottle, ready to pour himself another drink, he paused as the woman's words haunted his mind. He had been befuddled before, and he did not need to be so again. Pushing the bottle away, he got to his feet and made his way outside, grateful for the lanterns that lit the deck.

The Lieutenant was busy shouting orders to drop anchor for the night, the crew working hard so that they could go to their bunks and rest. It would give him the perfect opportunity to get the woman up to his quarters without being spotted.

Marching back below deck, he tried not to feel the slight warmth curling through his veins as he thought of his previous encounter with her. Dismissing the memory, now tarnished, he cleared his throat as he peered through the gloom, seeing her still slouched in the corner with her hat over her eyes. He tried not to let his gaze travel over her legs, her breeches molded to their shape.

He coughed again, but there was no response. "You there!" he exclaimed, rattling the cell bars. "Don't tell me you're sleeping!" He could hardly believe it when she jolted awake, stretching a little before getting to her feet. Clearly, her confinement was not concerning to her in the least.

"Did you need something, Harrington?"

Gritting his teeth, Thomas pulled the key from his pocket. "It's 'Captain' or 'sir,' thank you."

She rolled her eyes, pulling the bandana from her face. "What's your plan, Harrington?"

Irritation had his jaw clenching, but he kept his voice even. "You'll come to my quarters."

"Very well," she murmured, moving closer, "and what will you tell the crew?"

"I haven't got that far yet," he muttered, swinging the cell door open. "But I will not allow them to believe that we have not captured Captain Adams. I'm finished with chasing him. That part of my life, that *torment*, is over."

She paused, no smile on her face as she looked into his

eyes. "You have struggled to catch him, that is for sure," she replied, softly. "But, if you would listen to me, I believe I have a plan that might allow your crew to believe that he is gone from your watch once and for all."

Thomas studied her face, aware that she was not laughing at him but rather held a serious expression. "Why would you want to help me?"

She laughed now, shaking her head at him. "Do not think for one moment that I wish to help you, Harrington. This is for the good of my — of Captain Adams' – ship. If he is supposedly gone, then we need not fear the Navy chasing us." She tipped her head, "At least, not for a good few months or so. It's a winning situation for both of us."

Thomas did not want to ask for her help, but his mind was so troubled with everything that had gone on, he did not know what else to do. "Very well," he said, stepping aside so that she might move out of the cell, but staying close so she could not try to run. "What do you propose to do?"

"Have you a sack or two? Something heavy?" Pulling off her coat, she handed it to him. "Apparently Captain Adams has died in the brig. You will have to throw him overboard."

A swift realization took hold as he watched her remove her hat, reverently running her fingers over it for a brief moment before handing it to him. The hair he remembered so well was tied back in braids to keep it away from her face. He also could not help but notice without her oversized coat just how womanly her figure was, even if she was clad in breeches and a shirt.

"Are you going to help or stand and gawk at me?" she asked, frostily.

Flushing, Thomas dropped his head and turned to search the dark corners of the ship for a couple of sacks as well as something to fill them with.

Grasping two gunny sacks, he practically threw them at

her, before looking for an old cloth of sorts. He hated that she had noticed his perusal, even worse that he had allowed his eyes to linger on her curves. *She is a pirate,* he reminded himself. *And, for whatever reason, has allowed Captain Adams to use her in order for him to make his escape.* A mixture of embarrassment and frustration twined itself through his muscles as he finally found some sandbags, pulling two back toward her, trying to rein in his temper. She was, after all, providing him with the solution he needed.

"That will do quite nicely," she said, pulling a small knife from the corner of her boot. For a brief moment, Thomas thought she might come at him with it, but as he started toward her, she flashed him something of a humorous look before ripping the sandbag apart.

Thomas simply stood aside and watched as she filled the coat with sand, before buttoning it up. It was only then he realized that she had somehow found an old hammock, and was beginning to tie it up.

"Might you put the other sandbag at the end, where his feet would be?" she asked, wiping one hand across her forehead.

Grimacing, Thomas did as she asked, catching the way she pulled one feather from Captain Adams' hat and placed it within the confines of her shirt when she thought he wasn't looking. It was a strange gesture, and Thomas kept it to think on later.

"Very good," she said, eventually. "Your Captain Adams is quite dead and ready to sink to the bottom of the sea."

He grunted, refusing to thank her.

"Shall I slip away to your quarters now?" she asked, propping one hand on her hip and tilting her head to give him something of a coy smile. "Or do you have other plans for me?"

His body responded immediately to her suggestive tone,

forcing him to turn away. Marching to the steps, he flung open the trap door. "Thankfully, I know it is too dark for you to attempt to sail away, otherwise you would remain here in the brig until I decided to return for you."

He stormed up the steps and, seeing no one on deck, whispered for her to follow. Within minutes, she was in his quarters, and Thomas let out a long sigh of relief, before shouting for the Lieutenant and the first mate. It was time to dispose of Captain Adams.

CHAPTER 12

*E*leanor couldn't help but gape in astonishment at the opulence of the captain's quarters. Not only was it larger than she expected, but every piece of furniture was made of dark, mahogany wood. It was nothing like her own cabin on the *Gunsway*. In one corner of the room sat the captain's bunk, although it looked more comfortable than anything she had slept on before. It even had four posters, so that he might draw the curtains around himself as he slept. Large windows to her left looked out across the sea, with a welcoming window seat in front of them. A writing desk stood to one side. Wandering over to the window seat, Eleanor sat down and tried to ignore the frantic beating of her heart.

She had enjoyed toying with Captain Harrington, pretending to sexually advance on him to gauge his reaction. As much as she hated his mandate, there was something about him that perplexed her. During their first encounter, she had felt his soul, deep inside, yearning to be free of the hold of the Navy — and perhaps his society in general. She supposed his rage was a mask of his true emotions.

She had to admit that she was proud of her plan to trick the Navy out of their chase of Captain Adams. She hoped that also meant the *Gunsway* would be free from Harrington's dogged chase, which would cause her vast relief. It had wrenched her heart to give Harrington her father's hat, but it was necessary so that there would be no doubt over Captain Adams' supposed death. She had ensured that some of the famed hat was visible through the hammock, one feather poking out. The other feather she had kept for herself, although she hoped that the captain had not seen her take it, for she wouldn't want him to question why it meant so much to her. She felt it tickle her skin just below her collarbone and had to fight a sudden rush of tears. She hoped Harrington would not discover the truth -- that Captain Adams was truly gone from this world and that he had left her behind in order to continue the *Gunsway's* captaincy. She must get back to her ship — and soon.

The door suddenly flung open and the captain stomped inside, his blue eyes searching the room until they landed on her, sitting comfortably with her legs up on the window seat as she stared out the window.

"Did you manage it?" Eleanor asked, turning to him and trying to sound as nonchalant as possible. "Is your fight at an end?"

In response, the captain flung down his hat and shrugged out of his coat. "It is done," he said, tersely, his strong cheekbone twitching.

"Good, I am glad to hear it," Eleanor replied, airily, "although that does leave you with a problem."

He growled at her, pouring himself a large glass of brandy.

"What are you going to do with me, Captain?" Eleanor asked, rising to her feet and walking over toward him. "Are you going to throw me overboard as well?" She arched one eyebrow, refusing to acknowledge the thump in her chest when his eyes met hers. She had not failed to notice how his gaze had lingered on her curves, and had decided to use his interest to her advantage. In truth, she still found him quite a handsome man despite his tight, angry features. His forehead seemed to be permanently furrowed, while fine lines bordered his eyes and his strong jaw was held tensely. Not that any of it mattered. The only thing she had to focus on was finding a way off this ship.

"I will think about that come the morning," he replied, and she wondered if that was humor in his voice. "But, first, you are going to give me some answers." He slammed his empty glass down and walked back toward the door, locking it tightly and pocketing the key. "We will not be disturbed."

Eleanor ignored him, pouring herself a brandy before settling back down in the window seat, crossing one leg over the other as though she was there for a social call, hoping she appeared unaffected by him.

"Answers," he said, crossing his arms over his chest as he stood in front of her.

Taking a small sip of the brandy, Eleanor looked up at him smugly with a courage she did not quite feel. "I hardly think that it is fair to be so demanding, *Harrington*," she murmured. "Perhaps you might answer some questions I have too. An answer for an answer, what do you say?"

He gritted his teeth and she saw his hands clench. "You are in no position to bargain."

She laughed. "Oh, but I believe I am. No one else knows that I am here, do they? And, if they discover it, then questions might be asked about who exactly was thrown overboard – and why you allowed it." She lifted one eyebrow. "Answer my questions and I will answer yours." In truth, Eleanor would only answer what she wished to and would simply lie about the rest — although Captain Harrington did not need to know that. She was quite sure that his answers, however, would be the truth and nothing less. It was how he had been trained and she was sure he considered himself an honorable man.

"I could ensure that you swing from the gallows," he growled, bending down so that his face was close to hers. "I will declare that you are a pirate, and then you shall—"

"A — a pirate?" Eleanor whispered, contorting her face into a mask of fear as she pretended to make her defense to some unknown judge. "Oh, no, sir. I'm not a pirate. The captain, he took me to his bed but I did not please him. He lost his temper and now thinks that he can do with me as he will…." She trailed off, her eyes darting around the room as she continued her charade. "You might ask the barman in the tavern. He saw me with the captain. Captain Harrington, he kidnapped me and kept me in his cabin like a prisoner."

As his eyes widened, she grinned, pleased with herself. "You see? No one will believe you. Hanging a woman would not bode well for you. After all your years of failure, perhaps people might think that you've begun to lose your senses."

Inwardly, she congratulated herself on her victory as he stepped away from her before beginning to pace back and forth across the small cabin.

"I should throw you overboard," he said, stopping and turning to her, his eyes darkening as he stared at her. "You do not make the rules, miss!"

She just laughed at his frustration, knowing that she had him right where she wanted him. She was actually beginning to enjoy herself, although she felt rather sorry for him. He wasn't going to be throwing her overboard anytime soon and certainly wasn't about to take her back to Port Royal and attempt to push her toward the gallows.

For one, no one in his crew had seen him capture a female pirate and, secondly, it would be *far* too easy to play the part of terrified wench who had been used by the captain. He knew it as well as she. She had to hope that he might decide to simply set her down on an island somewhere. She had the resources and skills to ensure her survival until she could hail a passing ship or somehow make her escape.

"Very well," the captain said, sighing in defeat, pulling back a chair and sitting down. He had the decanter of brandy in his other hand and proceeded to pour himself a large measure. "Ask your questions. But swear you will answer mine – truthfully."

Eleanor tried not to laugh, schooling her features into a calm acceptance. "Of course I will," she replied, wondering if Harrington was truly so gullible.

"First," he began, his eyes darting away from her for just a second, "what were you doing in the tavern?"

"In Port Royal, you mean?" she asked, trying not to allow her own rising embarrassment to show. "Perhaps I was simply looking to take my pleasure."

"And you coincidentally found me?" he replied, raising his eyebrows. "Don't lie to me. You knew who I was."

She lifted her shoulders. "Perhaps I found you a singularly attractive man, Captain. It was nothing more than that."

He snorted. "You are lying to me again. I know I must have told you something of my plans as regards the *Gunsway*." His flush deepened. "I had partaken of a little too much liquor."

Eleanor smiled as she glanced at the brandy he currently held. "Yes, you did indeed, Captain. For what it is worth, you did speak to me of your plans for the *Gunsway*, but your words were mostly colored by disappointment and failure."

As she spoke, Eleanor studied him and was surprised to see him glance away, before dropping his head to stare at his hands for a brief moment. Apparently, his dismay was greater than she had realized. Pushing away the jolt of sympathy in her chest, she cleared her throat and prepared to ask her own questions.

"Why were you so eager to follow through with my plan, Harrington? Why so willing to pretend that Captain Adams is truly gone from this world?" She sat forward, her eyes boring into his as he raised his head. "Have you no honor?"

He slammed his glass down and rose to his feet with such force that his chair fell to the floor with a clatter, making her jump. His eyes blazed with passion, his face burning.

"I have more honor than someone like you will ever know," he ground out, his voice shaking, his emotion greater than she had seen from him thus far. "I have chased Captain Adams for years, receiving nothing but mockery and laughter in return for my troubles. Over and over he has outsmarted me, and I am finished with it." His voice slowly faded, and she could almost see the anger draining away from his face. "The Navy has refused to allow me leave from chasing that man," he finished, pouring another brandy. "I cannot bear it any longer. Perhaps I didn't think this plan through, for it will all come to naught when Captain Adams reappears. But the plan worked for now."

Eleanor sat quietly as she watched the captain. He pulled up his chair and sat down once more, before putting his legs up on the table and crossing them at the ankle. He held the glass of brandy between his two hands and stared broodingly at her. She could tell he was going to be deep into his cups once again, but perhaps that was to her advantage.

Eleanor's sympathy for him grew slightly despite herself. He had said near the same when he had taken her to his bed back in the tavern, but she had not realized how deeply trapped he felt. She was more than aware that he had not intended to share so much of himself with her, but at least it gave her something of an advantage. She could use that shame and embarrassment to her benefit. A pang of guilt, an unfamiliar sensation, wrenched her heart for a moment, causing her to frown.

"You see, Miss," the captain began, his voice now hoarse with emotion. "You have no idea what you have done to me in pretending to be the very man I have sought for so long. Yes, I agreed to your plan and yes, Captain Adams is now, for all intents and purposes, at the bottom of the ocean, but that does not hide the fact that I know the truth. I know he is still out there, and at some point, the Navy will too." He looked at her, letting out a long sigh, his blue eyes capturing her in their gaze. "Why did you keep that feather?"

She frowned, his question sending her off balance. She hated that he had seen her moment of weakness. "Captain Adams would want me to keep it."

"Why?"

"It is of sentimental value," she replied, not daring to give more away. She studied his handsome features in the lamplight, seeing the strain on his face as he put his head back against the chair. Clearly, his burdens weighed heavily. "Surely now, Captain, if you are free from chasing Captain Adams, you might be given some new task. Is that not enough to lift your spirits?" She did not quite know why she asked such a thing, or why she even cared. Perhaps it was the look on his face or the slump of his shoulders. Regardless, she waited until he raised his head to look at her, the fight gone from him completely.

"I will never be free," he murmured. "Never allowed to sail where I want, to explore uncharted lands or make up my own crew. I will always be at the Navy's bidding," he snorted and drained his glass. "I joined His Majesty's Navy so that I might escape my family's expectations, only for them to continue to pile upon me from not only my family but the Navy as well." His eyes took on something of a glazed look.

"It appears no matter where I go or what I do, I shall never be my own man."

Eleanor's heart clenched, seeing him as a man in despair instead of a haughty, proud Navy man.

"Sometimes, freedom is a choice we have to make ourselves," she said, softly. "Sometimes, honor is being true to our own heart and not what others wish upon us. What is your given name, Captain?"

He lifted his empty glass to her. "Mr. Thomas Harrington, second son of the Duke of Ware." His eyes began to close even as he attempted to remain focused on her. "And yours?"

"Eleanor," she replied, without thinking.

"Eleanor," he repeated, his eyes now firmly closed. "What a name for a pirate."

CHAPTER 13

*T*homas awoke with a thundering headache, his muscles stiff from sleeping in a wooden chair. He momentarily lacked memory as to how he had found himself here. It was only when he saw the empty glass on the table beside him that it all came back to him.

He had thrown "Captain Adams" off the ship, pretending to the crew hands that the man had collapsed, red spots covering his body, before he had stopped breathing. That had forced the men to follow through with his intention of getting the body off the ship almost at once, afraid that there might be some terrible sickness aboard the ship if they did not. And now he was faced with the problem of a tempting, young, female pirate named Eleanor on his ship and in his cabin.

Frowning, he tried to rise, aware that a blanket had been placed over him. Where was she?

It was barely light, and he struggled to make out his cabin in the gloom. She was not in the window seat where he had left her. Scrabbling at his pocket, he let out a long breath of relief as he felt the door key through the material, relieved that she had not attempted to escape. Not that she would have been able to either, given the dark clouds that had surrounded the ship for most of the night. She would need the stars to guide her if she were to escape in the dark.

Leaning heavily on the chair, he looked around only to spot a figure lying in his bed. She had certainly made herself comfortable in captivity — but then he caught sight of that pale blond hair spread out across the pillow and a fiery warmth began to overwhelm him.

She was exactly as he remembered her from the tavern, and memories of how she had felt under his hands surged to the front of his mind. Her chest rose and fell, her eyes tightly closed and lips slightly parted. She had clearly removed her braids for sleep, and the waves they left through her hair made him want to run his fingers through it. A strange desire to press his mouth to those lips almost had him staggering toward her, but instead, he sat back down in the chair and simply watched her.

Eleanor had been quite right when she'd laughed at his suggestion of putting her into the hangman's noose. He would never have been able to do such a thing, but at the time, he had been able to do nothing other than threaten her in the hope that she might answer his questions with honesty. His anger, now that he had time to consider it, came from a place of confusion over his emotions. He hated that she had given herself up in the place of Captain Adams, but he equally despised the sensations growing in his chest whenever she smiled at him. He also respected what she had done, and the courage her actions had revealed. She was smart, witty, and bold.

He wanted her.

Shaking his head, Thomas let out a low groan. He could not have such feelings for a pirate, and especially not a captive. Her words to him, while made in jest, were too close to the truth for him to be truly comfortable. She *was* his captive, and he was holding her in his quarters, against her will. What was it about her that had him feeling such things? He could have nearly any woman he chose, a woman who would be proper and upright, who had moral fiber and followed the law of the land... but that was not the kind of woman Thomas wanted.

For that kind of woman was exactly what he had left behind, what the Navy offered him now: staid and boring, rules and regulations the driving force behind it all. Were he to marry a woman like that, she would ensure she produced the heir and the spare, just in case the worst was to happen to his brother, before requesting that she have her own set of rooms in the house, or moving to the country and living her own life. He had seen it time and again. That was not what he wanted.

He desired fire and passion, and the night he had spent with Eleanor, although it had been short and was somewhat hazy, had been exactly that. She was unlike any other woman of his acquaintance, and he could not help but be drawn to that. This was a woman who represented all he longed for in life. Hell, she had even *tasted* like freedom.

"She is a pirate still," he muttered to himself, getting to his feet and walking over to the bed to look down at her. His hand reached out of its own accord and picked up a tendril of her hair, rubbing it gently between his fingers before letting it fall. She was a puzzle. She knew how to raise his ire — she rather enjoyed it, he realized — yet she had a caring heart as well. Despite everything, she had been kind enough to remove his boots, place a blanket over him and had then gone to sleep herself, albeit in his own bed. A pirate, yes, but a compassionate one.

He shook his head and stepped back. That did not add up, for pirates were hard-hearted mercenaries, without conscience. *At least, that is what you have been told,* he reminded himself, moving toward the window to look out at the horizon. The sun was only beginning to rise, the first orange beams shooting up into the grayish sky.

His thoughts wrapped themselves around him until he almost lost himself in his daydreams.

"It is quite beautiful," said a soft voice, startling him. He looked down to see Eleanor, her hair unbound and wild around her shoulders, looking out across the sea to where the sun was slowly rising. "I shall never become tired of watching a new day begin."

Thomas did not know what to say, his heart stopping in his chest as he saw her hair pick up the light of the sun, giving it a fiery glow. Her skin was lit with gold, as the soft smile on her face showed just how much she appreciated the glorious sight.

It seemed strange that a pirate would care about such a thing as beauty, but he refused to dwell on it any longer. Instead, he simply kept his face turned toward the sea, watching the sun rise above it while his pirate captive stood next to him, so close that her shoulder brushed his arm. Gooseflesh rose on his skin, hidden by his shirt, as they stood together in silence. He wondered, briefly, if she felt anything akin to what he was struggling with, hoping that, if she did not, she would not guess what it was he felt. He could not allow himself to dwell on such emotions, however, knowing that he had to somehow get rid of her without permitting her to re-join her ship — as unlikely as that was. No matter what he decided to do, he was sure that she would somehow find herself back on the *Gunsway*, back with Captain Adams. He still needed to know how she had ended up with such a crew. His heart sank in his chest as he thought of her departure. But he could not exactly keep her captive here forever, especially when his men could not discover her.

"I will be returning to Port Royal," he said, softly. "It will take us a few days. Once we are there, I will decide what to do with you."

She looked up at him, and Thomas' breath caught as her eyes met his. They were lit with the sun's flames, and heat seemed to emanate from them, washing over him like a river.

"You are not going to hang me, then?" she asked, quietly, a small smile tugging at the corner of her lips. She had seen his empty threats for what they were.

Shaking his head, Thomas shifted his gaze out the window before turning back toward her face, open and inviting. The anger and frustration that had filled him only yesterday already seemed to have vanished, taken away by the woman next to him. She seemed softer this morning, her mockery and sarcasm vanished. It was as if she had been holding that up like a shield, but it was no longer needed.

"In truth, Eleanor, I do not know what to do with you," he answered gruffly. "My path has always seemed so clear, but now…" He did not know why he was being so honest with her, but he found he could do nothing less.

He couldn't help himself. He reached a hand out, stroking a finger down her soft cheek. When she didn't recoil from his touch but, rather, leaned into it, he took her chin in his hand, leaned in, and kissed her soft lips. The kiss began slowly, tentatively, but when instead of refusing she pressed into him, he took more, his tongue teasing open her mouth before tangling with hers. What began as an unspoken desperation soon turned into something more, something tugging at him from deep within. He ran his fingers through her hair, brushing it back away from her face, as he forced himself to finally let her go.

Eleanor leaned back, and their eyes locked as they took one another in.

"Perhaps your path is too strict," she said, quietly, stepping back and turning to look out of the window once more. "*We* sail wherever we please, do whatever we wish."

The magic of the moment broken, Thomas snorted and stepped away from her, walking back to his table to put distance between them and keep himself from reaching out to her again. "You are pirates. You have no agenda aside from your next plunder."

"Do you think pirates are all so very bad?" she asked, coming to perch on the table, right next to where he was sitting. "Are we truly all as terrible as you believe us to be?"

Sitting back in his chair, Thomas tried not to look at her lithe figure, his brows knitting together with the effort. "The Navy would not be seeking to capture and hang pirates if you were not all causing such harm." Seeing her brows lift, he rolled his eyes in frustration. "Pirates take what they wish and use it for themselves. It is not right."

Eleanor studied him for a few minutes, her mouth settling into a firm line. Thomas knew he had offended her, but tried not to allow guilt seep in. He knew he was right. Pirates needed to be removed from the seas.

"You are quite wrong, you know," Eleanor murmured, eventually. "Captain Adams would only steal from — that is, he steals from those who do not need their treasure or came by it dishonestly, and he takes some of his wealth and gives it to the less fortunate."

Thomas wanted to snort with derision but held back.

"I can see that you do not believe me," she murmured, quietly. "Why not put it to the test, Captain? You are a man of truth and honor, are you not? Perhaps if you asked at the ports, you might discover that not all pirates are as you think. Only recently, Captain Adams handed out wealth to those in Arwenack Castle, keeping enough back to pay the crew's wages for the next quarter." She leaned a little closer to him, causing his heart to beat a little quicker. "You know, deep down, Captain Harrington, I believe you are envious of the life we lead."

Her words sliced through him, his entire body growing as cold as ice as he stared back at her. He did not want to admit it, but there was a modicum of truth in what she had said. Pirates had the freedom to go wherever the captain chose to go, pursue what they wished. It was a life he longed for, but one that would always be out of his grasp. He might have run to the Navy, but he was still a nobleman.

"You are quite wrong," he replied, getting to his feet and pushing the chair back. "And do not think for one moment that I intend to let you go back to the *Gunsway*. I will keep you on board here if I have to." Seeing the sudden fire in her eyes, he walked away from her, pulling on his coat and reaching for his hat before unlocking the door and stepping out onto the deck.

Upon securing the door's lock, he pocketed the key and strode out into the cool morning wind. Looking up at his ship's colors, he drew in a long breath, telling himself that he simply could never allow any kind of jealousy to grow. He had to hope that, now the Navy thought Captain Adams was no more, he might be allowed to choose his next commission. That would give him some kind of freedom, would it not?

Sighing to himself, Thomas dropped his eyes and stared across the sea. He could not rid himself of what Eleanor had said, the stories she had told him about Captain Adams and his supposed generosity. Would it be wrong to seek out the truth? To discover if, perhaps, these pirates were somehow different than what he'd expected?

"Where to, Captain?"

Turning to the Lieutenant, Thomas put his hat a little more firmly on his head. "Arwenack Castle, Taylor."

"Sir."

Watching the Lieutenant depart, Thomas swallowed his indecision away, settling his shoulders as he grew a little surer of himself. He would find out whether the pirate girl spoke the truth or not.

The only question that remained was, what would he do if he discovered her words to be true?

CHAPTER 14

Their course was now charted for Arwenack Castle back in England. Thomas was focused on a group of islands far to the southeast when his Lieutenant called to him.

"Captain, there's a ship coming quickly. You best come take a look. I believe it to be the *Gunsway*."

"They're likely here for their Captain," Thomas said, taking a look through the spyglass to confirm his lieutenant's assessment. Normally he would be ecstatic to finally have the ship in his grasp, but now it was a disastrous turn of events. If Captain Adams and his crew managed to board his ship demanding the return of a girl, any career he had remaining would be sunk. He'd be the laughingstock of England.

"Are they in range?" He asked his lieutenant.

"Yes, sir."

"Fire the cannons. In the meantime, prepare the men for battle. The *Gunsway* would have to be foolish to board us, but prepare nonetheless."

As his crew ran about the deck to challenge the *Gunsway*, Thomas prepared himself as well. Was one woman enough for the pirates to risk their ship for? Captain Adams had never challenged him in the past, and he hoped it wouldn't take much to make him turn and run this time. He didn't want to have to tell Eleanor that he had sunk the ship along with its crew, but he didn't see any way around it. As a captain in the Royal Navy he couldn't very well let the *Gunsway* sail right up to his ship.

The naval vessel shook as the first of the cannons fired. The ball landed just shy of the pirate ship, and Thomas ordered another charge. The *Gunsway* might have been smaller than his ship, but it was wily, and continued to evade the cannon fire. One cannon ball nicked the side of it, sending wood chips flying, but Thomas knew not much damage had been done. As the pirate ship neared, Thomas thought of Eleanor, alone in his suite with the cannons blasting. He ran through the ship down to his room, unlocking the door and charging in, only to find her fully dressed, one of his own hats perched atop her head. She looked every bit a pirate as the men currently coming after him.

"It sounds like you are about to be attacked, Captain," she said, a grin on her face. "Might I have a weapon?"

"Certainly not!" he exclaimed. "A pirate ship is approaching, it's true. Not to worry, we'll easily keep it at bay. I'll lock the door so that whatever happens, no one will come in and hurt you. I have the only key."

He shouldn't have been surprised by her laughter. "Harrington, no one will be hurting me today," she said. "You've clearly never seen me in combat. Which ship approaches? Perhaps I have some knowledge that would be of use."

He evaded her question. "I can't have you fighting alongside my men, and I will not give you a weapon for fear you'll slit my throat. I shall return when they've gone. I came down here simply so you wouldn't be fearful of the cannons, but I see I need not have worried."

"You have a lot to learn about me, Captain Harrington, if you think some cannon fire would scare me," she replied. As he was halfway out the door, she spoke again. "Tell the *Gunsway* crew I shall see them soon."

He paused, decided not to engage with her, and continued on his way, locking the door behind him as he returned to his crew.

* * *

ELEANOR LAUGHED to herself at the shock on Thomas' face as he left the room. But of course it was the *Gunsway* returning for her, although she was annoyed that they had not followed her orders to run. It did, however, show their loyalty toward her and for that she must be grateful.

She had meticulously searched the captain's cabin for something to aid in her escape. Earlier this morning she found pieces of metal she was able to manipulate into a tool of sorts. Instead of picking the lock, she was going to remove it, along with the handle. She had a good start to her task, but now she returned to it in earnest, anxious to free herself and return to her crew. She heard the cannons fire again as she worked diligently on the door. Luckily, the captain had been too preoccupied to notice anything amiss.

The handle finally began to loosen as she heard the sound of boots hit the deck above her head. Her men had landed. She smiled in triumph as she wrenched the lock free and let herself out of the room. She took a look back at the cabin, surprised at her wistfulness of leaving this Navy captain whom she had hated as he had so doggedly pursued them for years.

She made her way to the deck, staying in the shadows of the rigging. Morgan was standing on the deck, negotiating with Thomas.

"Return our captain and we will leave you be," he said.

"Impossible," Thomas responded, seemingly confused at the demands of the first mate. "Captain Adams is dead, the body thrown overboard."

Morgan looked about to run his cutlass right through Captain Harrington when Eleanor caught his eye from the shadows behind Captain Harrington. She shook her head, then nodded to the sea. Catching her meaning, Morgan bowed his head and murmured, "How unfortunate. What, pray tell, occurred?"

Thomas explained the infection that had overcome the captain in his version of the events as Eleanor made her way to the side of the boat. She heard Morgan asking for pardon and a peaceful exit, as the *Gunsway* had not actually attacked the British ship, but instead had requested admittance.

She heard Thomas relent, to the dismay of his crew, as she shed her clothing down to her breeches and shirt. When the pirates began the return to their ship, she climbed the rail and dove into the water below.

✻ ✻ ✻

THOMAS WAS RETURNING to his chamber when he heard the splash. It was nearly silent, but it came from directly below him beside the rail. He immediately knew the cause — it was her. How the hell she had escaped from the room, he had no idea, but he wasn't about to let her go. He looked over the side to see her making quick strokes toward the awaiting *Gunsway*. She was a strong swimmer and would be gone quickly. Before he considered anything else besides catching her, Thomas threw off his coat and hat before diving in after her.

She heard the splash, and looking behind her, saw him in chase. She increased her pace. She was a quick, skilled swimmer, but he had placed his dive well and was that much stronger, and soon bore down on her, linking an arm about her waist.

"Let me go, Harrington," she cried, fighting against him. "It's best this way."

"Not today, Eleanor," he said, knowing she was right but unable to answer even himself as to why he had pursued her as he worked to keep them both above the surface. He lost his breath for a moment when she kneed him between the legs, but he managed to keep them afloat. "I need answers from you first."

He pulled them to the side of the ship, where the ladder awaited. He pushed her up ahead of him. "Up," he said, "and signal your crew. When you've answered my questions satisfactorily, I'll release you in due time. I'm not a cruel man, and I won't let you hang."

There was no hiding her from the crew any longer. They had gathered along the rail, astonished at seeing their captain hoisting a body out of the water.

Eleanor looked down at him with one eyebrow cocked.

"And how, Captain, am I to know I can trust you?"

"Because, Eleanor," he responded, quietly now. "I hold honor above all other virtues, and my word is my bond. Even to a pirate."

They reached the top of the deck, his crew gaping at her.

"The lady fell from the pirate ship," Thomas explained to them. "She'll be our hostage for the time being. She will stay in my cabin and there will always be a guard on her door."

She lifted his hat from the deck floor and waved it over her head at her crew, who responded with a glint of sunlight off a glass. The crew had been together for so long there was no misunderstanding their codes to one another.

She turned to him. "Very well, Harrington. I will answer your questions, with one caveat." She nodded toward the tiny dots of land shimmering in the distance, barely visible, almost no more than a mirage. "I see we're only a few days away from Arwenack Castle. Visit the port, and find what I'm telling you of Captain Adams to be true."

He nodded. "Fair enough."

Together they returned to his chamber. He shook his head in disbelief when he saw the doorknob hanging off the side of the door. He sighed, ran his hand through his hair, and kept Eleanor with him while he summoned a crew member to fix the door handle. Thomas declined to provide the sailor with an explanation as to what had happened to it. When it was repaired, he locked it behind him and walked to the deck to assess the crew.

When he returned, Eleanor was perched on the window seat, a space he was beginning to think of as hers.

"Good day, Captain," she said with a wry grin, "such a pleasure to host you in my chambers."

"Eleanor," he responded warily, sitting down opposite her. "Are you ready to answer my questions?"

"Aye, sir," she said with a mock salute.

"Where is Captain Adams, and how did you end up on my ship?" he asked. "I was fully prepared today to have Captain Adams himself demanding the return of a young lady. I thought my entire naval career was in ruins. And then a crew member boards my ship looking for its captain."

In truth, he had accepted his forthcoming demise with much less angst than he would have expected. True, he felt guilt at the shame he would bring his family but besides that he had felt… free. Then the *Gunsway* crewmen had come on board and completely shocked him — enough so, that he let them leave.

Eleanor chewed her lip. It was apparent how highly Thomas regarded truth and honor, but she couldn't very well tell him her father was dead and she was now the captain of the *Gunsway*. It would put him in a dilemma of what to do with her, and she didn't want to risk him keeping her prisoner.

"The captain came up with a plan and chose not to tell the rest of the crew about it," she said. "He told them he was surrendering himself, but I offered to go in his place. We left the *Gunsway* at the same time, me to your ship, and he to another location that he did not share with me."

He eyed her with suspicion. "I'm not sure I believe this tale."

"Believe it or not, it's your choice, Harrington."

"And who are you to the *Gunsway* crew and Captain Adams? I do not think it's regular practice, even for pirates, to have a woman on their ship, let alone to use her as bait."

"It's not regular, Captain, but it's been known from time to time," she responded with a smile. "Pirates, it seems, are much more accepting of women aboard than the Navy. Captain Adams found me as a girl. My mother was a prostitute and no longer wished to have me in her care. The captain welcomed me to his ship as part of his crew. He made sure I have always been treated with the utmost respect."

It was a partially true story — Eleanor simply left out the fact that the captain was more than just a kind soul but, in fact, her true father.

Thomas appeared conflicted, like he wanted to believe her but knew, in his heart of hearts, that she could spin a tale as easily as tell the truth.

"Now Captain," she said, "you will continue to make for Arwenack Castle?"

"I said I would," he responded, "and I shall."

"Do you see the islands to the northeast?"

"I do," he replied. "In fact, I was intrigued by them when we caught sight of your crew."

"What would you say about a little day trip? You talk of freedom, Harrington. Let me show it to you. I know those islands well and can give you a taste of what life looks like on the other side. The lush vegetation, the waterfalls, the beaches, the nearly uninhabited land — when will you ever have another opportunity to explore such a place, with someone there to guide you?"

He eyed her warily. "I'm assuming this is part of an elaborate escape plan you've cooked up."

"Not at all. I trust in your word, and you say you'll release me. I also want you to visit Arwenack before I take my leave of you."

He rolled his eyes at her belief she could leave whenever she chose.

"Just a few hours, that's all I ask. I would so love to have time out of this cabin, as luxurious as it is, and you have made the deck off limits. We can leave in the early hours, when there are few of your crew awake."

He knew he should say no. It was a terrible idea, one which would more than likely lead to her escape. However, what would she do on an island on her own, without any means of transportation? If she chose to stay there, then so be it. Rationally, he knew he should say absolutely not and keep her on this ship, but her words of adventure called, and his heart swayed him.

Before he knew what he was saying, the words came out of his mouth. "Very well, Eleanor. We leave shortly before dawn."

CHAPTER 15

*E*leanor woke early the next morning, just as a hint of the sun began to break over the horizon. She stood over Captain Harrington as he slept, cramped in the window seat. She didn't suppose there were many captains in His Majesty's Navy who would let a prisoner sleep in his bed while he folded himself into a tiny, uncomfortable space – even if she was a woman. It mustered a twinge of gratitude toward him.

His face was still somewhat tense as he slept. She didn't suppose he was particularly comfortable, and she wanted to run her hand over his face to smooth away the lines covering it. Instead, she poked him in the side and he woke with a start.

He reached for his sword before his startled blue eyes came to rest on her as she leaned over him.

"Good morning, Harrington," she said with a grin. "Are you ready?"

She was looking forward to sharing the island with him, she realized. For once, she really was telling him the truth. She simply wanted a day out of this cabin before they sailed the rest of the way to England, and she chose the best way to bribe him, with the adventure he apparently so longed for.

* * *

HE SPLASHED water on his face to wake himself up before making his way to the kitchens to prepare food for the day. As he stuffed it into a sack, he shook his head at himself, still unsure of this scheme of hers.

Before they left, he laid down rules.

"Eleanor," he began, "if we are going to do this, you must agree to a few of my stipulations."

"Aye, Captain," she said, mocking him.

"I am serious about this," he said, crossing his arms. "If not, back to the ship it is, and then not onto Arwenack Castle, but to London, where I will turn you in as a pirate."

"I believe we have covered that, Harrington," she said.

"Yes, but now my crew has seen you, and knows you came from the *Gunsway*," he replied. "You would still have a chance, but not as great a one as you would have had before."

She appeared to consider this but with a shrug brushed it off.

"Now," he continued, "you will stay at my side at all times. No wandering off. You will have no weapon. And should we encounter anyone on the island — any living person at all — you will have no contact with them. Is this understood?"

"I can agree to those rules, although I believe it would be in your best interests if I had a weapon. You never know what creatures may approach."

"Absolutely not. If the need should arise, I have a gun and a sword and will deal with the threat accordingly."

"As you wish, Captain," she said nonchalantly. "Now lead on before the morning is too far upon us to depart."

He led her down the ship's deck to where the rowboats

waited, realizing as he did so that she now knew the exact escape route — although he suspected she would be perfectly capable of finding it on her own.

He had ordered the crew to anchor a few hundred yards from shore, telling them the woman was going to show him a treasure stash. He sighed as he realized she was making a liar out of him.

"Bending the truth," was her response when he argued with her on the story. Now as they began the short row to shore, he had to marvel at the strength in the sinewy muscles he could see through her white blouse. He mused anew that he had never before encountered the likes of her. In his life, women seemed to fall into one of two categories — the "marrying kind" his mother enjoyed pushing upon him, and the "non-marrying kind," who neither expected nor wanted anything from him. Upon their first meeting, he had incorrectly branded Eleanor as the latter. He realized how much he must have drank that night to have thought of her so. Looking at her now, one could never make the mistake of thinking her something cheap.

She caught his gaze and a corner of her mouth lifted. "Enough with the daydreams, Harrington. Put your back into it and pull your weight."

He didn't respond, but kept time with her and ensured he outmatched her pulls.

They reached the sandy shore and hauled the boat high enough so that it would be safe from the incoming tides. She brushed the sand off her hands and turned to him with enthusiasm.

"I do not believe I've ever had the pleasure of escorting a guest through this island," she said. "Come, I'll show you one of my favorite places. My — Captain Adams introduced it to me many years ago and it's where I always long to return. It feels like home, nearly as much as the *Gunsway*."

She led him through thick brush, the rich, lush greenery surrounding them as she found the nearly invisible path through the jungle-like island growth. He had seen this type of natural vegetation before from the beach, but had never taken the time to immerse himself in it. The sun filtered through the trees, over the jagged mountainous cliffs that lined the other side of the island. This was a different world, one that filled him with peace and contentment.

Walking ahead of him, her hair blowing in the gentle breeze, her hands trailing through the grasses, Eleanor seemed like part of the island herself. She belonged here, was one with it.

This, he thought to himself, this was contentment. For the first time in a long time, he felt whole – and it had taken a pirate to show him how.

SHE GLANCED BACK AT HIM, smiling at the way he lifted his face to the sun with a soft smile on his lips. She had felt this spirit within him, but had been curious to see if it was truly there or a figment of her imagination. But here he was. Beneath the layers of anger, of frustration, and a general dissatisfaction with his life, lay this man. A man who did not belong in the Navy, nor polite society. He had the soul of a pirate; he just didn't know it — or didn't want to admit it.

She led him up the side of the gentle incline in silence, although the birds and the animal calls on the wind spoke volumes. She turned them left to another path, one which broke through the trees into what looked like a clearing up ahead. He could hear the gurgle of water, and as they rounded the corner, she stepped out of the way to let him take in the sight for the first time.

It took his breath away. The water cascaded over a rocky

outcrop to fall into a pool of water below. The water was an emerald green from the reflection of the trees, while a sandy shore surrounded the pool, a rainbow of exotic flowers encircling it as if they had been planted there in a pattern by God Himself.

She saw the reflection of the sight in his eyes, the way he responded with admiration and appreciation for all that nature held in store for them.

She finally broke the silence and the spell. "Come, Harrington," she said. "The walk has been warm, and I would love a swim."

She could sense his shock as she quickly stripped down to her undergarments. "It's not as if this is something you have not seen before," she said with a laugh. "But I will leave on a layer to protect your modesty."

She began to climb up the rock face to the top of the outcropping.

"Is that safe?" he called up to her. "How do you know if this pool is deep enough to dive?"

"Because, Captain," she said, "I have dived off this rock face too many times to count, and have explored the depths of this pool."

With that, she raised her arms overhead and dove cleanly into the green below, disappearing beneath the surface. She broke through the water, laughing.

"My, but that feels wonderful. Come, Captain. Join me this time."

* * *

As she walked out of the water, her thin layer of clothing stuck to her skin, it was all Thomas could do to keep himself from removing that layer from her as well. He shed his shirt, but left his trousers to keep from embarrassing himself as he followed her up the cliff wall. He stood at the top, looking out at the forest below. After she dove in again and cleared the surface, he followed her, the thrill of adventure shooting through his veins as he sprang off before the cool water engulfed him.

He came to the surface with a laugh on his lips, turning his head to find her bobbing in the water next to him.

"You're a good swimmer, Captain," she said. "I've heard many of the English nobility would drown should they find themselves in this predicament."

"There is a lake on my family's estate," he explained. "My brothers and I learned how to swim from the groundskeeper and his children. It's a skill that has served me well, it seems."

She began to swim back to the shore when he caught her arm, holding her above the surface.

"Eleanor," he said softly, injecting a note of seriousness into his tone, "thank you for bringing me here."

"You're welcome," she replied with a bit of lilt to her voice. "You are the first I have shown this place to. In truth, I do not know why I brought you, but I felt it may speak to you as well."

He didn't respond, but pulled her in with one arm, the other holding them above water as his strong legs kicked below. He took her mouth with his, kissing her deeply, drinking her in as if she was the one giving him life. She responded eagerly as she had before, a willing partner of fire as the cool waters lapped around them.

She groaned and wrapped her arms around his neck to deepen the kiss, her fingers threading themselves in his hair as her legs wrapped around his waist to bring herself closer to him. He gripped her tighter as they began to slowly slip underwater, her passion overwhelming him. She finally broke away as they both came back to the surface, gasping for air.

They swam to shore as one, but before he could say a word, she shushed him, one finger on her lips. He looked at her with question, and she cocked her head over to the right. Grabbing her clothes, she motioned for him to follow her into the brush as she pointed ahead.

There, children ran through the trees in the distance. They were minimally dressed, and, he realized, inhabitants of this island. They laughed as they jumped over tree roots and followed a well-worn path. Minutes later, their mothers followed, some carrying babies, others foraging along the path as they went.

When they were well out of sight, he turned to her.

"Did you know these islands were inhabited?"

"Of course," she responded. "I had thought they were keeping to the other coast of the island, but perhaps they have moved. We have an understanding. We barter with them, and they allow us to visit the islands now and again, leaving us in peace."

"The children, they seem so..." his voice trailed as he sought the word. "Happy."

"Of course they are happy," she said. "Why would they not be?"

He shook his head, unsure.

"You must do something for me," she said quietly.

"What's that?"

"Never tell anyone about this place. About what you've found here, about this island. The British, they have a propensity to take over, and I do not want to be the reason these people would lose their home or their way of life."

He slowly nodded, agreeing with her. She angled her head and subjected him to a long assessing stare, perhaps not believing him. Finally, a smile spread over her face.

"Are you hungry?" he asked her, changing the subject. "Perhaps we should eat before heading back to the ship."

The thought of returning filled him with dread, but this was an escape, a day away. His life awaited him, whether he liked it or not.

THEY HAD DRESSED, eaten, and were retracing their steps back to the beach when crashing through the brush behind them signaled something approaching. They both stilled.

"What do you suppose that would be?" he asked her warily.

"I'm hoping…" She turned as suddenly the wild boar broke through the grasses, approaching them at a fast pace.

"This is why I need a weapon," she called to Thomas, who didn't respond, but pushed her behind him as he calmly stepped in front and neatly killed the boar with a fatal strike of his sword.

"Well," she said, impressed, "I didn't know you had that in you, Harrington."

"I didn't become a captain only because of my family's connections," he said, laughing at her incredulity. "Ye of little faith. I do have some skills to my name."

She nodded her assent.

"It's not the pig's fault we were here," he said. "We were trespassers on this land, and I'm sorry he died for it."

Was this the same man she had met in the brig just days before? Eleanor wondered to herself. Had she been surprised at his actions, she was incredulous at his depth of feeling for the animal.

"Well, Captain," she said. "I can assure you, there are many more where that came from. Shall we not return it to the ship? It will feed many of your crew over the next day or two."

He nodded his assent and picked the boar up as they

returned to the boat, still where they left it, high on the beach.

"You know, Harrington," she said as they rowed back to the ship. "You're not such a bad sort, for a Royal Navy Captain."

He laughed at that. "And you, Eleanor, are not such a bad sort for a pirate."

"You enjoyed yourself today, did you not?"

"I did."

"This is what freedom tastes like. This is what piracy affords you — the chance to do as you please, to take breaks from life when you need them. Do you see why I live the life I do? Why we all do?"

The spell of the day was broken as she brought up the pirate life. She could tell from the darkening expression on his face.

"I understand what it offers," he answered in a soft voice. "But there is still the trade off for this life with lying, thievery, and the murder that comes with it." He shook his head. "It's not worth it, Eleanor. I have morals. I have honor. That, you will never understand."

"I understand better than you will ever know," she said. "Continue for Arwenack Castle. I cannot wait to hear what you find there."

Silently assenting, he nodded, and later that evening, she sat in his quarters, watching as he charted the course.

CHAPTER 16

The nights on the return were tortuous. Ever the gentleman, Thomas continued to sleep cramped on the window seat. Eleanor claimed it was ridiculous considering their previous encounter, but he insisted. Between the window seat and knowing she was lying in his bed just feet away from him, it had been difficult for him to get any sleep, but he refused to touch her again, while the gap in the way they lived their lives lay between them.

Now, Thomas strode through the port at Arwenack Castle, his eyes roving over the street beggars. For once, he'd dispensed with his usual uniform, although it was strange to be walking through the town without his hat. He simply did not command the same respect.

Clearing his throat, he addressed one of the beggars, who turned lazy eyes on to him.

"You there, what do you know of Captain Adams?"

"Captain Adams?" the man replied, his countenance brightening almost immediately. "Is he in port?"

Thomas shook his head, registering the disappointment

that flickered over the beggar's face. "You do know him, then?"

The man frowned and held out his hand. Thomas pulled a crown from his pocket and handed it to him, noting just how thin the man was.

"Captain Adams is good to us," the man explained, biting down once on the coin with dirty teeth, ensuring that it was genuine. "He shares his wealth with us. No one else helps us except him."

Thomas' frown deepened. "He's a pirate."

"And a good one at that," the man retorted, pocketing the coin. "He always returns with more gold. Who else would give us coin and ask nothing in return? No one. No one cares for us."

Thomas shook his head. "That's probably because many of you would waste their generosity on drink."

The man's face grew shuttered, his dark eyes becoming almost black as he glared at Thomas. A chill washed over the captain as he took a step back, realizing his error.

"You know nothing of Captain Adams," the man sneered, settling back against the wall. "He'll know if you spend his gifts on drink or on whores. If that be the case, you won't get another penny from him."

"How does he know?" Thomas asked, trying desperately not to believe the man. When the man didn't respond, Thomas gave him another crown, only for him to cackle with laughter.

"Captain Adams has eyes and ears everywhere," he replied, grinning wickedly. "If he don't want to meet you, then you will never lay eyes on him." Lifting one eyebrow, he stared insolently at Thomas. "And, Captain Harrington, I don't think Captain Adams will be anywhere near this port. He'll know you've arrived. You are one person he most certainly does not want to meet."

Thomas turned on his heel and stormed away, hating that, despite his lack of uniform, the man had easily recognized him. Apparently, he could not be invisible here. He tried again with a few others, most of the interactions repeating the first.

Walking back toward his ship, Thomas stopped between some barrels and tried to get his thoughts in order. What the beggars had told him was a reflection of the information Eleanor had imparted. There was no way for her to get word to this port, and certainly not to these specific people. Which meant only one thing.

What Eleanor had said was true.

Thomas shook his head violently in an attempt to dispel the thought. He did not want it to be true, for that would change what he had always believed about Captain Adams — and about pirates in general, he supposed. Adams had slowly become less of a brute and more of kind-hearted man right before his eyes, and Thomas hated it, for it meant the past three years had been a senseless pursuit of a good man.

He did not want to face Eleanor again, not now. He had too much to consider but, given that the ship would be leaving again in the morning, he had very little choice. Besides that, he still had no idea of what to do with her. Thomas made his way out from among the barrels and back toward his ship. He would stay on deck for as long as he could before retiring for the night. He just had to hope that Eleanor would be asleep by then.

Unfortunately for Thomas, it was not to be so.

* * *

ELEANOR SIGHED HEAVILY as she sat down at the table, her stomach rumbling. Harrington had been gone for most of the day, and she had not eaten a single thing since breakfast.

It was now well past retiring hours, and he still had not returned to his cabin, even though she had heard his voice on deck a few hours ago. She had stared through the window to look at the port, wondering if there was any way to signal for help, but had eventually given up. He had said he would release her, and she believed him – for now at least. Should he not hold true to his promise there would be plenty of opportunity for escape. At the moment, there was still some crew on the deck and she could not simply smash a window and dive out into the water. The chances of her being caught were far too high.

Finally, the lock turned and Harrington walked in, his eyes widening slightly as he saw her waiting for him.

"Where have you been?" she demanded, thumping her fist on the table. "Are you intending to starve me to death?" Attempting to rise, Eleanor had to sit back down in her chair as a wave of weakness washed over her, from hunger as well as sitting in one place for far too long.

"Sit, please," Harrington mumbled, rushing to her side and helping her to carefully sit back down. His face was red as he stared down at her, apparently a little alarmed over the lack of color in her face. "I do apologize, Eleanor. I didn't want any of the crew coming in here alone with you. Let me go and fetch you something now."

"Fill the plate!" Eleanor replied, not pleased with her weakness in front of him. He rushed from the cabin, leaving the door unlocked.

Eleanor eyed it for a moment, wondering if she should take the opportunity to escape to the deck and find a way off the ship.

But she dismissed the thought, as she was far too interested in what Harrington had discovered at Arwenack Castle. Had he spoken to someone who had told him of Captain Adams' generosity? Were his thoughts on pirates changed in the least? And why did she care so much about what he thought?

He was back within a few minutes, a tray of food in his hand as he made his way through the door. Putting it on the table, he glanced at her in surprise. "You didn't try to escape, then."

Eleanor didn't answer, reaching for a hunk of bread the moment it was put on the table.

"I thought you would have," he said, shrugging out of his coat and flinging his hat onto a chair. Sitting down opposite her, he watched with a slight smile on his face. "That's the second thing I've been surprised about today."

Choosing to satisfy her stomach before her many questions, Eleanor ate the warm stew, bread, and then an apple. Finally, her stomach stopped grumbling and she caught the captain's eye.

"What was the first thing that surprised you?" she asked, watching him carefully.

He drummed his fingertips against the table. "I didn't want to believe you, but it seems you were telling the truth about Captain Adams."

Eleanor struggled not to let the triumph she felt show on her face. "I told you so, Harrington."

"Thomas," he murmured, staring into her eyes. "Call me Thomas."

Surprised at his sudden willingness to allow her to call him by his first name, Eleanor nodded, running his name over her lips. "Thomas, then."

"I don't understand," he said softly. "What I learned today goes against everything I know. Why did His Majesty's Navy force me to seek a gentleman pirate for so long, when I know there are others out there — bloodthirsty, cruel men — who I could have caught instead?"

Troubled eyes met hers, making her inwardly wince for

the struggle he was going through, even though she didn't want to feel anything for him. There was a vulnerability about him, hidden beneath the layers of naval training, that was beginning to shine through. He was showing himself to be a very different man from the one who had laughed in her face in the brig.

"You don't like it here," Eleanor found herself saying, seeing the confirmation in his eyes. "You want to be free, but the Navy has you bound. Even if you have some freedom now to choose what you will do next, you will always be bound by their laws, their way of life. It's not the freedom you've been searching for."

He shook his head, a grimace on his face. "And you think pirating is the answer."

It wasn't a question, more of a statement, but one with which Eleanor could not help but agree. "Your perceptions of a pirate's life and character have already been changed," she murmured, tentatively reaching across the table to brush his fingers with hers. "Why not consider your own life?" She felt him start as she touched him, but he did not move his hand away. Without his navy hat and coat, he seemed more like an ordinary man, one who was struggling with his thoughts and his decisions.

"You need not be a pirate, Harrington," she continued, quietly. "Just as Captain Adams did not have to be one of the cruel, bloodthirsty pirates you talk about. You also, however, need not be a navy captain. Why not buy your own vessel? Hire your own crew? I know you have the wealth to do so, given your background. Why stay here?"

He did not answer her for a few minutes, simply looking down at her hand where it lay on top of his as though seeing it — and her — for the first time.

"Honor," he said, quietly, "my family requires honor. I could not bring them scandal."

"You have sisters, then? Brothers, perhaps?" she asked, wondering who he was speaking of. "Surely leaving the Navy to seek out your own way of life cannot be too much of a scandal."

"I have four siblings. An older brother, a younger brother, and two sisters who are not yet married," he replied. "The scandal would still affect them all, in some way."

Eleanor managed to contain her scoff of derision, although she did roll her eyes. "Honor," she repeated, pushing her chair back and getting to her feet, "can be defined in many ways. It can be living the life your family has chosen for you, sure. Or it can be living the life that is calling to you, one that is worthwhile and betters the lives of others."

He remained where he was. "This is all I have," he said as sorrow filled his features. "This life is all I know."

"Then make a new life!" Eleanor exclaimed, rounding on him with blood pounding in her ears and her heart beating a staccato rhythm. "Forget about scandal and do away with propriety! Listen to your heart and make a decision for yourself. That is the only true way to find freedom."

She watched him as his face grew a little more open, losing the tension that had ravaged it only a moment before.

"Think of it," she whispered, perching herself on the table and looking down at him. "Think of the freedom to captain your own ship, the way the wind will chase your sails as you make your way by the stars." She could almost see his body loosening, his eyes growing lighter. "No heavy coat, no proud hat atop your head. Sail where you please and do what you wish. You might not be a pirate, but you are still a captain, free to be your own man." Before she realized what she was doing, she reached out and caught his face in her hands, aware of the slight scratch beneath her palms.

"Tell me truthfully, Thomas. What is it that's stopping you?"

He did not answer for a long time, simply staring at her as though she'd revealed some marvelous truth to him that he'd never heard of before. Eleanor found she could not drop her hands from his face, reveling in the feel of his rough skin beneath her fingers. His eyes were brighter than she'd ever seen before, even though they were lit only by the lanterns dotted around the cabin.

"Eleanor," he whispered, his voice breaking the silence, "why do you torment me so?"

She opened her mouth to respond, only for him to push himself up from his seat and catch her lips with his, plundering her mouth with a fiery abandon that had her clinging to him with a desperation she hadn't known she'd felt.

Do you want this to happen? she asked herself, as his lips tore away from her own and nipped down her neck. She could barely breathe, certainly could not think clearly, as all she knew in that moment was that she desperately wanted Thomas Harrington.

He had made himself vulnerable to her, opening up to her, letting her see him as a man instead of a captain. There was more to him than she'd first realized, and that knowledge had dug its way into her heart and planted itself there, spreading roots of affection right through it. Her fingers dug into his hair as he lingered on the soft spot just below her ear, sending shivers through her.

She needed him — and she was no longer holding herself back.

CHAPTER 17

*T*homas was no longer in control of his actions, as the haze of emotion and need swirled through his mind and body. Eleanor was warm and willing, returning his passion with such a fierce boldness that it stole his breath away.

She'd shown him a new outlook on life, forced him to reconsider all he knew — and that hadn't pushed him away from her. Instead, it seemed to loop around him and draw him closer, almost tying himself to her.

"Eleanor," he whispered, his voice heavy with need as he slowly began to unbutton her shirt, letting his lips trail hot paths across her bare skin. She shivered again and clung to him, her head thrown back as he pushed her shirt aside, tugging down the straps of the chemise she wore beneath.

Soon they were both entirely bared to one another, although Thomas couldn't have said how they had found themselves in such a state.

The lanterns flickered their warm glow over her skin as Thomas stepped away from Eleanor, holding her shoulders with his strong hands as he ran his gaze down over her. Her eyes were bright with a burning fire, her hands reaching for him.

The need for her crashed through him, pulsing straight down into his groin. This was more than just a physical passion – there was an innate call to him from within their souls. She was like the sea, tumultuous and terrifying, yet free and welcoming at the same time. She was an enigma, something he would never be able to truly understand but wasn't sure he could ever let go.

"Thomas," she murmured, her voice heavy with longing, "Thomas, don't stop."

When he released her shoulders, Eleanor stepped forward and twined her arms around his neck, pressing her lips to his. Thomas met her with a passion of his own, their lips clashing together in a furious desire. Their tongues battled for control as a fierce need to possess her overwhelmed Thomas more than any other desire ever had before. Boldly, she explored the muscles in his torso, as his hands ran down her back and grasped her bottom, her muscles there as firm as those in the rest of her body.

Thomas wanted to be in control, wanted to remember every moment of this. It could not be the same as last time, when he had been so beguiled with drink that he could only remember certain parts. He could not even recall how she had felt beneath him – but it would not be so this time. She did not seem to be concerned by his obvious desire for her, and he groaned in pleasure when she took him in hand.

"I know you want me, Thomas," she whispered in his ear, her strokes slow and leisurely, "won't you let me lead the way?"

With a growl, Thomas picked her up, forcing her to drop her grip and grab onto his neck. He would not allow her to dominate here, even though her strength and tenacity impressed him.

"We do this my way," he rasped, putting her down on the table. With a quick movement, he pushed the food and drink to one end, before stepping in between her legs. "Tell me you want me too," he managed to say, pushing her hand away as she reached for him again. "Say it, Eleanor."

Eleanor leaned back slightly, presenting her breasts to him as though she might distract him from the question. Closing his eyes briefly, Thomas clenched his teeth and forced his body to stay entirely still. He had to hear those words from her. He had to know that she wanted this as much as he.

"Thomas," she murmured, reaching forward and taking one of his clenched hands in his. "You are strong, with impeccable self-control. It must be the naval man in you." One eyebrow raised, her lips quirked upward, she apparently waited for him to take the bait.

With immense effort, he gave only his steady breathing in response.

"Very well," she sighed, perhaps unable to wait for him any longer. She shifted, moved as though desperate for his touch. "Yes, Thomas, I want you. I want this." She gazed up at him, vulnerability flickering in her eyes. "I shouldn't, but it seems that I cannot help myself when it comes to you."

Those were the words he'd been waiting for. With a groan, he began to kiss her once more as she wrapped her arms around his neck and pulled him closer to her, pressing her breasts to his chest.

"Eleanor," Thomas breathed, moving his hands down her shoulders to lightly touch her breasts. He was gentle with her, feeling a tenderness that he hadn't expected. She gasped at his touch before her eyes began to close as she threw her head back. His mouth took the place of his hands, which trailed down her body until he reached her core.

His touch elicited a startled jerk and a moan from Eleanor, causing heat to pour through him and pool deep inside in response.

Jaw set, Thomas lifted his face to hers. He would not take his own pleasure, but simply waited for her. She wasn't touching him at all, and his body was crying out for it, but her face registered sheer concentration and her muscles coiled, tightening like a spring.

"Kiss me, Thomas," she whispered, reaching one hand to his face and pulling him gently toward her. His hands moved to knead her breasts as he did as she requested, settling himself between her legs. Once there, he ceased all movement, although it took everything within him to hold himself back.

"Eleanor?" he asked, giving her the final opportunity to halt this before they went any further. Instead, she opened her eyes and smiled at him. At that, he could not wait any longer. Pushing into her, Thomas held himself in check, not wanting to rush this moment. He saw her eyes flutter closed again, as her mouth opened to expel a slight sigh. Slowly, he began to thrust, and with it came such an explosion of feeling, both physical and deep inside his chest, that he had to catch his breath.

Eleanor let out a long, languid moan, the table rocking beneath her slightly as Thomas moved within her. It was all the encouragement he needed, seeing her throw her head back and begin to move her hips in time with his.

His body burning, Thomas began to pump faster, the sensation almost ending him then and there. But no, he would wait. He was unsure whether Eleanor had experienced any kind of pleasure the last time they had been together, but this time he was going to be completely sure that she enjoyed this as much as he. He wanted her to always remember what they shared her together – no matter what came next for each of them.

"Thomas!" Eleanor gasped, her back arched against the table as he moved in quicker strokes, touching her core with his long fingers.

At his touch, Eleanor arched back, letting out a long, intense cry of bliss. Thomas pushed in once, twice, then let himself go, joining her on a wave of pleasure as exhaustion rippled through him.

"Thomas, that was… incredible," Eleanor whispered, her eyes still closed as she held herself close against him. "Whatever are we to do?"

* * *

ELEANOR PUSHED HERSELF CAREFULLY FROM THOMAS' bed, giving him one long look before reaching for the quill and parchment she'd seen on the writing table. Their coming together – this time – had been unlike anything she had ever felt before. Despite his surly demeanor and the fact that he was a nobleman and a naval captain of all things, she felt a connection deep between them, one that she didn't want to break – and yet there was only one way to move forward.

Writing him a letter seemed the best way to explain things, while giving him the option to return to her should he choose.

She could hardly believe what it was she was feeling for the captain. But that precise moment they had found release together, the way forward had made itself entirely clear, and it was only now that she was able to follow through. It was taking a risk, that was for certain, but Eleanor could not bear the thought of leaving him, never to see him again. She had seen him as he truly was, no longer swathed in the clothes of

His Majesty's Navy, and he had found his way into her heart. This was the only way to know for certain what he felt himself.

"Goodbye, Thomas," she whispered, putting the parchment where he would see it. "I pray you come back to me."

CHAPTER 18

*E*leanor picked up the key to the door, which had been sitting on the table next to where she had written the letter. Perhaps Thomas trusted her to stay or, more likely, it was now a clear sign that if she chose to leave, he was not stopping her.

She twirled it around in her hand, staring at it, wondering for a moment if she was doing the right thing. But this was the only way she would truly know his intentions.

Dressed, she let herself out the door, taking one last look at Thomas, spread out on the bed in a deep sleep. After they had made love, he had cuddled her toward him almost unconsciously, whispering love words in her ear.

The way he looked now tugged at her heart. He was peaceful in repose, free of the cares that weighed him down as a captain in the Navy. Should he not come for her, this is how she would choose to remember him, instead of the tightly wound, brooding naval officer.

She stealthily kept to the shadows as she found her way to the rowboats. She knew the *Gunsway* would be waiting in the caves near the port, and would be ready to sail once she boarded it. She was aware it had trailed them from afar, just out of sight, but close enough to watch over her. It was what she would have done had her father been the one captured.

She lowered the boat and jumped in without raising any alarm, but it wasn't until she was well out of sight that she felt truly safe, despite the dark ocean around her. It was a clear night and her father had taught her well. Using the coastline in the distance and the stars above for guidance, she followed the direction to the *Gunsway*. When it came into view, a sense of peace and belonging rushed over her. She was home.

The crew was ecstatic when she boarded the ship. Their respect for her had apparently grown following her decision to give herself up to the Navy to save them. Now her escape was another exploit that would be well remembered. Morgan joined her for a drink, and she recounted the entire experience — leaving out a few details.

"I believe, Morgan," she said in a pleasant tone, "that the days on the run from Captain Harrington may be over."

As he began to drink to her statement, she held up a hand to stay his action.

"He will no longer need to search for us as I told him exactly where we'll be."

He looked at her, astonished, before she explained, with a little more detail, Thomas' own desires, and the plan she had suggested to him.

* * *

THOMAS WOKE with a lightness in his heart. Before he could recall what had happened the night before, sensations of freedom and ease he had not experienced in as long as he could remember washed over him.

When last night's pleasures came back to him, he grinned

and rolled over for Eleanor, only to find an empty space in his bed.

His smile faded as he knew, without question, that she was gone.

The melancholy drifted back as he raised himself up onto his elbow and looked around him. Her clothes were gone, the key in its place but, he was willing to bet, the door unlocked. What a woman. She was wit and wisdom, fire and spirit. She was like no one he had ever met before. And she had chosen a life without him.

He didn't know how he would do it, but he vowed that he would find her and prove to her that he was worthy of her. It was when he rose from his bed and reached for his trousers that he saw the note, beautifully written on a piece of his own parchment. His heart beat faster as he read:

Dear Thomas,

Our meeting may have been unconventional, but I believe our paths have always been destined to cross. Your spirit, the one you keep so hidden beneath all of your layers of angst, is as free as the one I was born with. I urge you, Thomas, whatever you choose to do in the future, do not let that spirit be crushed, but rather, let it fly.

While our time together has been short, it has been, to say the least, memorable beyond belief. Should we not meet again, I will hold the time with you in my heart forever.

I have a confession to make. I have not been truthful with you, although I feel you know that already. Captain Adams, the pirate you have been chasing, was my father — my true father, who raised me after my mother did not want me. I grew up on the Gunsway, and have always been as true a member of the crew as any man.

My father died after our run in with the Savage Soul. I am unsure what ailment caused his death, but he died saving me from Captain Wayland. My father was a pirate, yes, but he was as good of a man as I will ever know. The tales about him are true.

He named me Captain as he died, and the crew honored his wishes. It was my decision to give myself up to you, and when the crew came to collect their captain, it was me they were looking for.

I did not wish to deceive you, Thomas, but you know I could not tell you the truth.

I am telling you now because of what I feel in my heart for you, and because it seems you have lost your way. You yearn for adventure, Thomas, for the love of the free and open seas, to go where you please and where the ocean takes you. Explore it with me, Thomas. Together we can see the world and everything it has to offer.

I am giving you something with this letter. I am giving you my trust. I would love nothing more than for you to join me, but if you chose not to, I ask that you not come after me. While I would give myself up once more if it meant saving my crew, I do not want them to be punished for a mistake I have made in sharing our location with you.

Join me, Thomas. Leave behind the trappings of the Royal Navy and become the man you were meant to be. I would be honored if you were by my side. Find us in the Iron Caves.

Love,

Eleanor

Thomas let the letter fall from his fingers and flutter to the floor. He had known she was a pirate but the captain! Captain Adams? Questions floated through his mind as the magnitude of her lies were made clear to him. She had spun story after story to him, from the moment they'd met in the tavern at Port Royal to last night, when they had fallen asleep after making love. But why? And how did she not hate him after the many years he spent chasing her, her father, and her crew?

She was a pirate captain. She was what people like him fought against. And he loved her.

CHAPTER 19

"*I* don't think he's coming, Captain," her first mate said, his words hesitant and compassionate.

Eleanor shook her head, refusing to give up. "It's been but three days."

"The crew are getting uneasy," Morgan replied. "Dropping anchor for such a long time in one place isn't the wisest choice."

Sighing, Eleanor dropped her head, knowing that the first mate was right. She'd been waiting and hoping for Thomas to arrive, to throw off the chains of the British Navy and come to join her in the water but, as yet, there was no sign of him.

"We will give it until sunset," she said, heavily. "Prepare the ship. We weigh anchor in a few hours' time."

The first mate shouted the orders, which were greeted with cheers from the crew. Eleanor's heart grew heavy as she stayed where she was, her gaze searching the horizon for any sign of a boat. Her eyes dimmed as she thought of how she had left him in the desperate hope that he would give up everything he knew to come and sail with her. He had wanted freedom, and she had offered it — as well as her heart. Perhaps she had been mistaken in that regard. Perhaps he had never truly felt anything for her, using her only for a physical release.

If she could, she would have stayed with him, but she knew there was no chance for them to be together in the life that he knew. He hadn't offered it to her, either because he didn't want to, or because he knew he couldn't.

"I'll be in my cabin," she muttered dully to the first mate, turning her back to the ocean – and to any chance she had with Thomas.

"Captain!"

A sudden shout stopped her just as her fingers wrapped around the handle of her cabin door. "What is it?"

"It be a boat!"

Her heart lurched, and she raced to the other side of the ship, peering out across the water.

"Eleanor!" she heard the shout echo across the ocean's surface, the boat nearing as Thomas' strong arms pulling the oars through the water. "Eleanor!"

"Help him aboard," she ordered, remembering just in time that she had to keep her head in front of the crew. "The minute he's aboard, everyone is to go below deck." Her eyes narrowed as she glared at the crew, not expecting anyone to question her. "This is to be a private conversation."

Maintaining her composure, she stood tall and waited for Thomas to climb on board, giving him a slight nod to let him know that, while she welcomed him, she had to wait until the crew were gone.

"You did not bring anyone with you, I hope?" she asked, as the last of her crew scurried away, listening to her orders despite their curious looks behind them as they went. "The Navy will not be appearing on the horizon?" Her heart thumped as she took him in. He appeared very different from the last time she had seen him, his shoulders no longer tight near his ears, his jaw relaxed, his face in repose – as though this was what he had been waiting for. Still, she didn't allow herself to hope, not yet, that he was here for her heart and not for her capture. Should he have come all this way only to take her away as a pirate captain, all would be lost – everything that her father had worked so hard for, gone because she had given her heart away and trusted the wrong man.

"Eleanor," he croaked, his voice breaking with emotion as he stepped toward her. "I did not think I would see you again."

"I see you found my note," Eleanor murmured, her resolve slowly beginning to weaken as she glanced over her shoulder to ensure there was no crew left on deck before allowing him to take her hand. Sparks shot through her as their fingers met, the longing in his eyes echoed in her own heart.

"I could hardly believe it at first," he admitted, shaking his head. "A female pirate captain? And the daughter of Captain Adams? I confess I wasn't pleased at the thought that you had deceived me – and I was equally as displeased to consider you putting yourself in such danger. There was a moment in which I wanted to burn the note, and everything that was in it." A rueful smile appeared on his face. "However, my heart would not let me."

She let out a long breath of relief. "You know why I could not tell you of my true identity? I did not trust you then."

"And now?" he asked, a hopeful look in his eyes.

Eleanor smiled, stepping back and dropping his hand. "You have left the Navy, have you not?"

He nodded. "I have. You are the only one who has ever been able to see into my heart. When you offered me freedom, away from the trappings of my life and my choices, I could not help but consider it – even though it went against everything I had been raised to know. Could I leave behind all that was expected of me? I never would have thought it, and yet… it became too much to resist."

"And what of your morals? Your commitment to your family? The scandal of it all?" she asked, remembering what he had said previously. "What changed?"

His smile became tender. "You," he said, softly. "The life you talked about, the life so different from my own, forced me to consider what it was holding me back. Yes, there might be some scandal, but my mother and father have the impeccable first son already." He lifted one shoulder. "I am the second son. My behavior, in time, will not matter all that much. Perhaps I will be a much better son and brother if I am happy with my lot in life. And I have begun to understand that being a… a *pirate* does not necessarily mean murder and plunder."

Eleanor grinned widely, even as she felt her heart might burst. She could barely believe that she had Thomas standing on her deck, the warmth in his eyes speaking to her in ways his words never could.

"What have you told your family?"

Thomas shrugged. "I wrote to them, stating that I was going out on my own adventure and expected to be a good many years at sea. I asked my father to arrange an honorable discharge for me. I ask nothing of the Navy – no retirement pay or purchase of my commission, as long as they release me." His eyes softened. "I did promise my mother I would write to her and visit when I could. Despite her constant nagging that I should marry, I know she worries."

"Of course," Eleanor murmured, remembering how much her own father had worried about her, even though she was as capable a pirate as he.

"I know I chased your father for a great many years," he continued, almost apologetically. "But I was doing as I was tasked and, in time, it became the sole purpose of my life. I thought that should I capture him, I would be able to find the freedom I'd been seeking for so long. It was only when I had you in the brig that I slowly realized the Navy would never allow me that, no matter how successful I was. I will never fight against the Navy. They gave me a home, they do honorable work, and many good men sail with them. But it's not the life for me."

Tilting her head, Eleanor let her smile spread across her face. "Then rid yourself of it," she replied, nodding pointedly at his heavy uniform jacket. "I see you have already dispensed with your hat."

Thomas drew in a long breath, closed his eyes and shrugged out of his coat. "I don't need this," he said, as though reassuring himself. "I won't be a part of that system any longer."

"Then throw it to the waves," Eleanor encouraged, stepping closer and taking his hand. "The sea will give you the peace you seek."

Together, hand in hand, Eleanor and Thomas walked over until they could see the depths of the water beneath. It was a calm day, with only a few breaths of wind, and the sea was quiet and still.

"Should you choose," she said, "I would not be opposed to seeking out a license to become a privateer, under a different name. To make us more legitimate, yet retaining our freedom."

He looked at her in shock. "You would do that?"

"If you are giving up your entire life, Thomas," she replied, "I should be able to change the way I do business."

When he looked at her, she could see the love she felt for him reflected back in his eyes.

"Throw it in, Thomas," Eleanor whispered, her hand tightening on his.

She dropped his hand and took a step back, knowing that this was for him to do alone. She saw the flickering emotions cross his face, the tautness of his features as he hoisted his heavy coat in his arms, before flinging it away from him with a shout.

Moving to the side, Eleanor watched as the coat — the last trappings of the British Navy — slowly gathered water and sank beneath the waves.

"You did it, Thomas," she murmured, watching it until the last part of it was pulled under by the water.

"I could not have done it without you," he replied, his voice husky as he turned to her and slid one arm around her waist. "You have brought me what I have been looking for."

Eleanor shook her head, seeing him in an entirely new light. "You are different now from when I first met you, and that has come about because you allowed yourself to be open. I believe it was your vulnerability — albeit liquor loosened your tongue and made you somewhat charming — that began to draw me to you."

"You still care for me, then?" he asked, turning so that he might face her. "Even though I am — was — a member of His Majesty's Navy? The man who chased your father?"

Smiling, Eleanor nodded. "It is very strange how the sea brought us together, but I will not deny that my heart is filling with love for you."

Thomas leaned down so that his forehead pressed lightly against hers. "I love you, Eleanor. I have to be by your side; otherwise, I might lose myself again."

"You must swear an oath of loyalty to me," Eleanor quipped, sliding her hands up and around his neck. "Each one of my crew has done so, and I cannot expect anything less from you."

He chuckled at the mirth in her voice, pulling her closer with a firmness that made her gasp. Heat rushed through her body, pooling in her core as his breath tickled her cheek.

"I swear it," he whispered, before lowering his head for a searing kiss.

EPILOGUE

*D*inner began as a somewhat silent affair, although none of them could take their eyes off of Thomas and his wife. His wife! Marie could hardly believe that her son had been married without her there to witness the event. Yet at least one of her children finally had married. That was something to be pleased about.

Eleanor wasn't exactly the type of woman she would have selected for Thomas. But she was beautiful and polite, Thomas seemed quite happy, and Marie could swear she saw a slight bump in the front of Eleanor's dress, signifying that a grandchild might finally be on the way. The couple was visiting England for a short time before returning home.

"Eleanor," said Violet, breaking the silence. "You must tell us all about how you met Thomas. We cannot wait to hear more!"

"Oh, it's not much of a story," Eleanor responded, staring at the dinner utensils in front of her. "I lived with my father in the Americas, and I met Thomas when he was in one of the ports. Unfortunately, my father passed soon afterward."

"I did want to marry Eleanor here, with the family

present," added Thomas, taking up the story as he took Eleanor's hand. "However, it would not have been proper for an unmarried woman to cross the sea without a chaperone, so we were married there, and then returned to inform you all in person."

"I still should have liked to have been present," sighed Marie. "I suppose we could perhaps have another ceremony. Now tell me, Thomas, why do you insist on staying at sea? I cannot believe that now you are not only putting yourself at risk every day, but you are doing so on a private vessel and not as part of the Royal Navy. You know your father will provide you with whatever funds you need to live your life."

"I know, Mother, but this is what I choose to do," he responded.

"And Eleanor?" she persisted. "How can you be happy living in a port town, at times on a ship?"

"I actually find it quite enjoyable, Your Grace," Eleanor responded with a winning smile. "Nothing quite speaks to me like being on the deck of a ship."

Marie still didn't quite understand. "You were just at the peak of your naval career, Thomas. You could have likely moved up the ranks to Admiral."

"I'm not sure that's a fair statement to make, Mother," Thomas responded. "Besides, I thought you were against me joining the Navy."

"Yes but a privateer… It just sounds so dangerous," she said. "Has Thomas told you of his successes, Eleanor? Did you know he captured the relentless Captain Adams, when no one else could?"

Thomas cringed at that, and Marie knew he must be embarrassed at her speaking his accolades, but she was proud of her son.

"Yes, actually, I am well aware of his capture of the dashing and daring Captain Adams," Eleanor said with a smile. "And when he captured the captain, he gained so much more than he could have imagined."

"Whatever do you mean?" asked Marie, wrinkling her nose.

"My apologies, Your Grace," Eleanor responded. "That must be a turn of phrase we use in the Americas. Needless to say, I am proud of Thomas and all he has achieved." She turned to look at her husband. "You, darling, are one of a kind."

"And you, my love," he responded, "are a one and only."

Thomas' face, now as kissed by the sun as Eleanor's own, was so much more youthful than when Marie had last seen him. The lines around his eyes had eased, and the stern look he had carried around with him had faded. He had found the freedom he had so longed for, not only in his new way of life, but in the love he had for Eleanor. It truly was lovely to see.

Polly, a hopeless romantic, appeared to be fascinated by both their displays of affection as well as the thought of living across the ocean. Like her brother, she was intrigued by the tales of pirates and the high seas, and Marie had to make sure she didn't get any ideas of her own.

"Eleanor," she said, "are you not afraid of pirates? What are they like? Are they frightening?"

Eleanor grinned. "I actually don't find them frightening at all," she said. "I find, for the most part, pirates are not all they are made out to be."

Marie's mouth dropped open, but before she could ask Eleanor how she would know such things, Thomas continued the conversation.

"Violet, sister, how is your search for a husband going?"

Marie rolled her eyes at her daughter's lack of motivation in finding a husband, and she didn't miss Violet shooting her brother a withering glare.

Thomas smiled, as content as Marie had ever seen him.

They had been shocked at his choices, true, but were happy for him and he remained the honorable man he had always been. The love of his life was at his side, a woman who loved him for whom he was, who had seen through the anger and bitterness to find the spirit inside that spoke to her soul.

And that made Marie as happy as a mother could be.

* * *

Dear reader,

I hope you enjoyed reading Thomas and Eleanor's story! I've always loved a female pirate, and had so much fun writing this true enemies to lovers tale.

Thomas has four siblings who are waiting for their happily ever afters. Keep reading for a sneak peek of Violet's story, or you can download it here.

If you haven't yet signed up for my newsletter, I would love to have you join us! You will receive Unmasking a Duke for free, as well as links to giveaways, sales, new releases, and stories about my coffee addiction, my struggle to keep my plants alive, and how much trouble one loveable wolf-lookalike dog can get into.

www.elliestclair.com/ellies-newsletter

Or you can join my Facebook group, Ellie St. Clair's Ever Afters, and stay in touch daily.

Until next time, happy reading!

With love,

Ellie

* * *

Clue of Affection
Searching Hearts Book 2

The boring life of a spinster takes a sudden turn when she witnesses a murder and suddenly becomes engaged to an earl.

Yet Violet Harrington has always vowed she would marry for no reason other than love – despite what her mother has to say about it. Little did she know a chance encounter in the gardens outside of a ball would change her life forever.

The Earl of Greville is not a typical peer, preferring adventure and excitement, which he finds by helping investigating criminal activity involving the peerage. But when the daughter of a duke becomes entangled in his current case, he must act quickly to protect her.

While the earl awakes dormant desires within her, Violet is horrified to learn of her betrothal through an announcement in the newspaper. Can Joshua convince her to marry him anyway, and together, will they solve the murder in the garden?

AN EXCERPT FROM A CLUE OF AFFECTION

iolet's fingers curled into fists, her nails digging into her palms through her thin white gloves. Was she well enough hidden where she was? How could she possibly escape? This Roberts – a murderer – had shot Sir Whitby, and was now wandering around the gardens to ensure that there were no witnesses to his actions. Violet did not have to wonder what would happen to her if he was to find her, for his callousness had been clear.

She could not leave the gazebo for fear that he would see her, nor could she remain here indefinitely. Yet she had to find someone, to tell of what she knew.

A sudden scraping sound had her heart racing, her hands going to her mouth to stop herself from crying out.

"Come on, now," came a low mutter, as someone stumbled into the gazebo. "Let's see you."

Violet sunk backward, unsure of the identity of the man, but aware that his voice did match any she had heard already. It allowed her to breathe slightly easier, although there still certainly the chance he was in league with the other men.

Staying as silent as she could, Violet watched as the stranger made his way to the side of the gazebo, bending low and peering out of the window as though he was searching for something.

"Not here yet," he muttered, obviously talking to himself, "unless I've missed them."

Her shaking had eased although hadn't stopped altogether as she wondered if this man was, perhaps, waiting for the players of the scene to arrive. He just didn't realize that he was actually too late. Violet did not know whether to make him aware of her presence, as she was still entirely at a loss to know who he was. If he discovered her there, would he try to silence her too? Or would he wish to help her? It was too much of a risk to take, so Violet chose, instead, to keep silent.

Unfortunately, the decision was soon taken out of her hands. The man crouched down before something clattered to the floor. He muttered curses under his breath, bending down further. Violet could not see him at all, the darkness at the bottom of the gazebo hiding him completely. She could hear him scrambling over the floor, searching for whatever it was he had dropped, although she suspected that he was trying to move as quietly as possible. Her pulse beat quicker, although she tried to breathe as shallowly as possible as the sound of his searching drew closer.

Without warning, a hand brushed her skirts, and it took everything for Violet not to let out a scream.

"Who's there?" the man growled, standing up. "I warn you, it will be the worse for you if you do not reveal yourself."

"Please," she whispered, her words ragged, "don't hurt me, I beg of you."

"Hurt you?" he replied, his voice a harsh whisper, likely

once he realized she was a woman. "Why would I do such a thing?"

Relief flooded her. "You are not with… with them?"

"I am not."

She took a breath, clasping her hands tightly in her lap. "Then might I ask who you are, sir?" Violet was not quite sure that she believed this gentleman was not associated with the murderers, for he had very evidently been aware of their presence this evening.

"Lord Greville," came the surprising reply, "and you are?"

"Lady Violet Harrington," she murmured after a moment's hesitation, unable to think of another response in her shock, although she was now convinced that this man was not who he said he was. Lord Greville was an earl, one she knew only by name and in passing, but certainly not a man who would gad about the gardens on a dark evening, in search of a murderer.

"Daughter of the Duke of Ware, then, I believe," the earl replied, keeping his voice barely above a whisper. "Whatever are you doing out here?"

Violet was not sure what to say, for, in that one sentence, he had at least proven his awareness of her family. Frustrated with the darkness that shrouded them both, she wished she could make out his features. Could he truly be Lord Greville?

"I might ask you the very same," she replied, feeling a little stronger now that she was no longer alone. "An earl on the trail of a murderer?"

His swift intake of breath told her that she had revealed more than she had realized.

"You saw them, then?" he asked, harshly. "When? Where? They killed a man?"

"Hush, please!" she whispered, loudly. "There is a man with a pistol searching the gardens this very moment, to ensure there were no witnesses."

He paused, evidently thinking over what she had to say. "Then he will not be the only one searching, for there are more of them," he murmured, after a moment. "This gazebo is neatly tucked away – indeed, had I not known it was here, I might not have seen it, since the darkness of the evening hides it so well. How did you come to find it?"

"I just... stumbled upon it," Violet could not help but shiver once more. "Do you think he will find me — us?" The bench creaked as she sat down upon it, suddenly very cold and frightened once more and needing its support.

"May I?"

Before she could respond, the gentleman stepped forward, attempting to sit down next to her. The bench was not all that wide, but he managed it somehow as she swept her skirts out of his way.

"You are cold," he murmured, sliding his jacket from his body. Warmth enveloped her as he pressed it around her shoulders, and she inhaled the scent of pine that immediately surrounded her, finding that it calmed her somewhat. "Let us remain here for a few more minutes and then, once I am sure that all is well, we shall return to the ball."

"I thank you," she whispered, fighting the strange desire to lean against him and place her head on his shoulder. "I will admit to being quite afraid."

She could feel his breath on her cheek as he dropped his head, whispering quietly in her ear. She shivered again, not from fright this time, but his breath against her neck.

"What was it you saw?" he asked. "Can you tell me in detail?"

Not wishing to recall the horrifying spectacle to her mind but understanding the need to, Violet closed her eyes and quickly sketched out the details, shuddering as she recalled how the smaller man's body had slumped to the ground, life gone from him in one quick moment.

"Could you identify the first man if you saw him again?" he whispered, hoarsely. "Think hard, Lady Violet. This is of great import."

"I – I do not know," she replied, softly. "I might be able to recognize his voice, although I do recall that the deceased man – "

"Sir Whitby," he interrupted.

"Yes, Sir Whitby," she continued, with only a slight shudder. "He did refer to this man as 'Roberts.'"

The answer seemed to satisfy him, for he looked away from her and did not ask anything else. Violet settled into his coat a little further, pulling it snuggly around her shoulders. Soon she would be back at the ball, and all of this would seem like a dream or a mystery novel.

"Come," he said, and held out his arm, leading her toward the door, bending suddenly to pick up a pocket watch, which must have been what he was searching for earlier.

"We must be quiet," he murmured, as they stepped out into the cold air. "The danger has not yet gone."

Violet swallowed her fear and let her eyes adjust to the moonlight. So far, the earl had proven himself to be trustworthy and certainly hadn't shown any sign of wanting to hurt her. She was still curious as to what he had been doing slinking around the gazebo, and why he was so interested in what she had seen. He seemed to have some understanding of what was happening — much more than she did. At the moment she was going to have to trust him, for she certainly could not return to the ballroom without his help.

"Wait!" he whispered.

They had not moved but two steps away from the gazebo when she saw him pause, tension rippling down his arm beneath the hand she had rested on it. Freezing as he held up a hand in a sign for her to remain silent, Violet did as she was asked and waited, wishing that her breathing was not coming so quickly but aware that she could not prevent her fright. Was someone coming? Had they left the gazebo too early? Her mind ran with images of what the man might do should he find them, for she was quite sure that he would act quickly without any regard to who they were or what they had seen.

In truth, it probably would not matter to him whether or not they had witnessed the murder, for he would not take any chances. If he had a group of men at his beck and call, Violet and the earl would just be another two unexplained disappearances, their bodies sent to the bottom of the Thames where no one might ever find them. Violet's pulse raced at her vivid imaginings.

Then, entirely unexpectedly, the earl turned around, wrapped both arms around her waist and pressed her back against the side of the gazebo, his eyes catching the moonlight as he looked down at her. Violet stared up at him, her hands flat against his chest, seeing his face for the first time. Briefly she noted eyes the color of cocoa, and a strong jaw with a hint of stubble under an aquiline nose. However, she did not have much longer to contemplate his face any further for, without warning, he lowered his head and kissed her soundly.

Violet stood there in shock as his hands pressed gently against her back. Violet struggled to think clearly as his kiss intensified, confused by why he had kissed her and just how she was supposed to respond.

Then, slowly, she began to feel a most unexpected sensation. It was a gradual, unfurling warmth that started in the pit of her stomach and began to spread itself all through her, right to the very tips of her fingers. Her hands made their way around his neck, and she threaded them into his hair as he angled his head to deepen the kiss. Whatever it was he was intending by this, Violet was already quite lost in all that it was bringing to her.

She did not know how long he kissed her for, her eyes remaining closed when he finally lifted his head.

"You are quite lovely," he murmured, capturing her chin in his hand. "Although I should apologize for my lack of propriety."

She gave him a slightly dazed smile. "Not at all," she murmured, the warmth that had spread through her now giving her the strength to stand without his assistance. She now had a few more moments to take her fill of his face, softened by the hint of a gentle smile. He was a good-looking man – not classically handsome, but intriguing. She supposed she had attended the same functions as him in the past. Violet wondered that she had not previously noticed him. His dark mahogany locks, slightly longer than was in fashion, had a slight curl at the ends, and Violet fought the itch to push back a few strands that had fallen over his forehead.

She watched as he bent to pick up his coat, which had slipped off her shoulders to the ground during their embrace. As he slipped it back on, she stood a little awkwardly, not knowing what to say, until he stepped back and held out his arm.

"We should return to the ball," he said, quietly. "You have been outside for quite long enough and I would not like to disconcert your mother."

Violet saw the way his eyes darted around the gardens, and she guessed at why he had kissed her. It was simply a ploy, to hide in plain sight. The warmth she felt evaporated at once, the slight smile falling from her lips as she took his arm.

"Of course," she murmured, dully, cursing herself for her

lack of sense as they walked through the gardens together, returning to the ball and her reality.

It had meant nothing. And she was a fooling for assuming otherwise.

* * *

KEEP READING Clue of Affection here!

ALSO BY ELLIE ST. CLAIR

Inventing the Viscount

Discovering the Baron

The Valet Experiment

Writing the Rake

Risking the Detective

A Noble Excavation

A Gentleman of Mystery

The Bluestocking Scandals Box Set: Books 1-4
The Bluestocking Scandals Box Set: Books 5-8

Blooming Brides

A Duke for Daisy

A Marquess for Marigold

An Earl for Iris

A Viscount for Violet

The Blooming Brides Box Set: Books 1-4

Happily Ever After

The Duke She Wished For

Someday Her Duke Will Come

Once Upon a Duke's Dream

He's a Duke, But I Love Him

Loved by the Viscount

Because the Earl Loved Me

Happily Ever After Box Set Books 1-3
Happily Ever After Box Set Books 4-6

The Victorian Highlanders

Duncan's Christmas - (prequel)

Callum's Vow

Finlay's Duty

Adam's Call

Roderick's Purpose

Peggy's Love

The Victorian Highlanders Box Set Books 1-5

Searching Hearts

Duke of Christmas (prequel)

Quest of Honor

Clue of Affection

Hearts of Trust

Hope of Romance

Promise of Redemption

Searching Hearts Box Set (Books 1-5)

Standalones

Always Your Love

The Stormswept Stowaway

A Touch of Temptation

Christmastide with His Countess

Her Christmas Wish

Merry Misrule

A Match Made at Christmas

For a full list of all of Ellie's books, please see
www.elliestclair.com/books.

ABOUT THE AUTHOR

Ellie has always loved reading, writing, and history. For many years she has written short stories, non-fiction, and has worked on her true love and passion -- romance novels.

In every era there is the chance for romance, and Ellie enjoys exploring many different time periods, cultures, and geographic locations. No matter when or where, love can always prevail. She has a particular soft spot for the bad boys of history, and loves a strong heroine in her stories.

Ellie and her husband love nothing more than spending time at home with their children and Husky cross. Ellie can typically be found at the lake in the summer, pushing the stroller all year round, and, of course, with her computer in her lap or a book in hand.

She also loves corresponding with readers, so be sure to contact her!

www.elliestclair.com
ellie@elliestclair.com

Printed in Great Britain
by Amazon